Sign up to Kay's mailing list to receive your FREE exclusive copy of the clean and sweet romance book *Songbird,* a Sunset Ridge Novella. You'll also be notified of new releases, giveaways, contests, cover reveals and so much more.

Get your FREE copy at subscribepage.com/kaywolfebooks

A voice and guitar. A song that will open doors. A fateful night that could end it all.

With her whole life uprooted - her high school love gone, her hometown left behind - Sarah Silver decides to start over again in the big city.

Her music is what has always been there to carry her through the hard times. Now, it's caught the attention of Nashville record labels, and of a handsome mystery man who is new in town and has come to see her play.

But one mistake can ruin everything. One decision can take it all away.

Will the sweet sound of the songbird remain,
when the storm has raged and gone away?

HEART OF THE MOUNTAIN

WILD HEARTS SERIES - BOOK 1

KAY WOLFE

FOX RIDGE PRESS

Fox Ridge Press

www.kaywolfebooks.com

BOOK DESCRIPTION

A broken heart. A mountain escape. Cougars, cliffs, wild storms... and a second chance at love?

Lara is a Chicago lawyer at a powerful firm. When the fallout from a failed relationship threatens to derail her life, a drastic change is needed. Her friend suggests a cabin-getaway in Wyoming to get her life in order. Suddenly, she find herself out west, the natural beauty beginning to heal her heart.

The mountains are no place for the unwary and one misstep can be fatal. When Lara is saved by Chase, she discovers in the ex-soldier a soul like none she has met before - a man who makes her feel alive again. Before she knows it, she finds herself on a journey that will risk her heart and her very life.

Can two hurt souls find love and healing during a storming Wyoming fall?

Heart of the Mountain is a moving sweet contemporary romance that is full of peril, heartache, romance, and redemption. It is perfect for reading by the beach or under your favourite tree.

This is Book 1 in the heartwarming Wild Hearts series set in the beautiful Wyoming mountains.

This book is dedicated to the brave men and women who have accepted the call of their country, and have been left forever haunted by the demons of their past.

May we never forget them in their time of need, for they stood up in the time of ours.

CHAPTER 1

Lara lifted her cup of coffee, but her hand was shaking badly and she spilled some on her fingers. She hissed with the pain and put it down, her brow creasing in frustration. She whispered a swear under her breath. She couldn't even drink a cup of coffee without it turning into a complete and utter mess!

Frustrated, angry, confused. Her emotions were all over the place.

"I'm sorry, it's just not working out for me."

Those were the words Craig had said to her the night before, and his replies to her questions had been little more than noncommittal shrugs that had frustrated and infuriated her. However, the reality of what was happening — another failed relationship, another dead end — had hit home.

She understood then why he had insisted on meeting at her place. He didn't want a scene in public. He wanted to make a quick getaway. That was exactly what he had done.

"Look, Lara," he said, standing up. "You're a great girl. You really are. And we had a great time. I mean it. But all good things must come to an end, you know? I just don't see it going anywhere. And I think it's time I look for something more serious. This was all a bit of fun. I think we both knew that was all it was going to be."

She glared at him, too angry, too choked with emotion, to respond. She spat out through gritted teeth,

"A bit of *fun?* Is that all I was to you? You think you can just... just... use me and toss me aside like that? How dare you?"

"Look, Lara. There's no need to get all hysterical now, is there?"

"Don't you *dare* call me hysterical! Who do you think you are? Get out!"

He'd sighed, shaking his head as though he were indulging a misbehaving child.

"Maybe we can talk again later. Once you've calmed down a bit. I think it's best if we just leave things for now. Goodbye, Lara."

He headed to the door, leaving her glaring after him, full of rage she could no longer articulate.

As the door closed behind Craig and it hit home that she was alone - once more, alone - the tears came pouring. Tears of sorrow, of anger, of frustration; all of it just overwhelming her and washing over her.

At work she was known for being strong. It wasn't easy being a female lawyer at one of the top law firms in Chicago. Although things had improved, being a woman in that world made things harder if one wanted to get ahead. She knew her looks didn't help. She didn't mean that with any sense of vanity, but she knew men found her attractive and she thought she looked great. At five and a half feet tall with long blonde hair, piercing, cold, blue eyes, and an amazing figure with curves in all the right places, she knew men's eyes followed her when she passed. There was no arrogance in it — it was simply a fact she was aware of.

She always dressed well - smart suits, skirts a suitable length, tailored outfits that didn't reveal too much but still accentuated her appearance, and never wore excessive makeup — but still had found it hard to be taken seriously when she first started out. However, through determination, hard work, and a tough, aggressive manner — both in the office and in the courtroom — she had earned a reputation she was proud of. She had earned her place at the table and the right to have her voice heard.

Yet, when she arrived home, closed the door behind herself, kicked her shoes off, leaned against the wall, and let out a long, deep sigh, the reality of her life was incredibly messy.

She seemed to have a knack for choosing the wrong men. That was her problem. Or maybe they chose her. Whichever it was, she found herself, time and time again, in these situations. She'd fall for some guy's sweet talk, things would seem to go well, she'd think that maybe this time, this could be *it.* But then the inevitable happened, and they ran. She never knew why. In moments of clarity, she realized it was them, not her. They were the wrong men for her. But those moments didn't stop her lying in bed at night, wondering what was wrong with her, what made them leave her.

Every time it happened, she would feel despair, this sense that her options were narrowing down, the years running down, and she could very well end up all alone. That was her fear, deep down, and the root of her despair. As she cried, her internal voice wailed, *why do I always end up alone?*

After those heart-breaking sleepless nights once the latest man had walked out, she would grit her teeth, grab her makeup, put on her war paint, and go to work. Go into battle. And that would help. She'd get deeply involved in a case and everything else would get pushed to the back of her mind.

Sure, she'd still have to deal with it all when she got home, but it helped the days to pass and as they went by, the nights began to get easier, and soon enough it was all behind her and she was ready to make another mistake. And she inevitably did.

She would get angry with herself about her bad choices, but she couldn't seem to break the pattern.

She spent the night after Craig left lying in bed feeling hopeless, empty. She cried, she pounded the bed with her fists in frustration, and she barely slept. All too soon the sun was peeking through her window and it was time for her to get up for work. She sighed and got out of bed. As soon as she did, the fatigue kicked in. She was lightheaded. She was angry with herself, with the whole situation. She had to be in court today. She couldn't show up as a shuffling, sleep-deprived zombie.

She got into the shower and stood under it for as long as she could, feeling a bit better. Then she looked at herself in the mirror. *Girl, you look awful,* she thought to herself, staring at the sleep deprived and emotionally wrung out face staring back at her. She did her makeup and hair as best she could, in the end deciding she at least looked presentable.

Then she headed to the kitchen of her chic downtown apartment with its fantastic views — that was what had sold her on the place, even though it had stretched her finances. She still thought it was absolutely worth it, anyway — and got herself a bowl of muesli and poured a cup of coffee.

When she lifted the cup to her mouth, the shaking had hit, and the physical and mental exhaustion thudded home. It wasn't just the lack of sleep. It was everything, all of it. Alone again. Even though she was only twenty-six, she still felt as though life was running away from her. She would tell herself that she had years, but what if those years to come were like the ones that had already gone? She didn't know what she would do then.

She took a deep breath and tried to think calm thoughts. She lifted her hand up and held it flat at eye level. It didn't look as though it was shaking too much now.

She picked up her coffee and drank it, letting the caffeine give her a much needed energy kick, at least superficially.

Time to face the world. Oh well, the day would be over soon enough. And then she would return to her empty apartment. But she couldn't think about that. She focused on the day ahead of her, the case ahead of her, the court appearance ahead of her.

Heading out the door, she made her way to work. Looking at the towering buildings around her, she thought about how much she loved Chicago. Even if times could be hard there, the city itself was a lesson in how things like that went — the winters could be harsh, and dark, and miserable, but the sun would shine again. The good times would come again. Sometimes when it was at its darkest, it was so hard to remember that, however.

She arrived at the office and walked in, smiling at Jenny, the receptionist, as she went. No matter how she felt, appearances were still important. Especially here. No matter what she did, there would always be those who saw her as "just a woman". Most of the people who held those kinds of views were the old senior lawyers in the company. Unfortunately, they tended to be the ones who held all the power, in particular the partners. So, she had to play by their rules, be better than the men she competed against, and most importantly, show no weakness at all. Sometimes that was the hardest thing to do.

She headed to her office to go over her notes and make sure she was as ready as she possibly could be for court later. There was a knock at the door. It was Mr. Peters, one of the senior partners. They had been working together on the case, and he was keen to make sure everything went according to plan.

"Good morning, Lara, how are you feeling today?"

"Fine, thanks, Mr. Peters. Just going over the notes one last time."

"Good, good. Best to be prepared. I don't want to put too much pressure on you, but how things go today could have a big impact on your progress in the firm. We've all got extremely high hopes for you."

"Oh, absolutely, Mr. Peters. I won't let you down. I promise."

No pressure. Yeah, right, she thought to herself.

He shut the door behind him, seemingly satisfied with her reply, and left her to it. She didn't have long before she had to be in court, so she had to go over the notes as quickly as possible.

The more she looked at them though, the more the words seemed to get jumbled in her head. *I don't know if I can do this,* she thought to herself, panicking.

But she laid her hands on her desk and breathed in and out deeply, again and again, until she felt better. *You've got this,* she told herself. Feeling more determined, she picked up her papers and headed for the door. It was time.

By the time she got to the courthouse, she was fully focused on the case. Nothing else penetrated her thoughts.

It was an intellectual property dispute. The company she

represented was an electronics firm, worth billions. Because of the number of parts, the different software, firmware, and hardware involved with their flagship products, they were constantly being taken to court by companies claiming some kind of intellectual property theft, or were taking other companies to court themselves claiming their products had been copied. Round and round it went, and it kept lawyers in business. These things were simple to settle — as should have been the case with this particular one — but companies always looked for the "white whale". That one case that would get them a multimillion-dollar payout and cripple their competition.

This was the side of the tech business that people didn't see at the slick conferences and product unveiling events. The corporate thuggery that took place in the courts. And there was a reason people didn't hear about it. That was because it wasn't particularly exciting. Also, in a lot of ways, it wasn't particularly pleasant. Besides gaining an advantage over rivals, it was also used to strong-arm smaller companies who might have come up with some interesting innovation. They simply couldn't afford to compete with the big boys in court and so they would end up selling whatever they had designed to the highest bidder or go bankrupt, watching all their capital run out as they fought a hopeless case in the courts. Either way, the big boys always got what they wanted.

Lara didn't find it particularly pleasant. It might be ethical, but the morals were questionable. Still, it was the career she had chosen, the career she loved, and if she had to hold her nose sometimes when she went to court and did things less than pleasant, then so be it.

When she arrived, a representative of the company met her.

James Montgomery. Monty, as he insisted on being called. Every time he saw Lara, he went in for a hug that was a bit too lingering, a bit too hands on for her liking. But she grimaced and got through it every time.

"Lara!" he said when he saw her, holding his arms out for the inevitable hug. Lara, however, had other plans. She'd grabbed a coffee on her way up to the courtroom and pointed at it. "Sorry, Monty, don't want to spill this!" He looked slightly disappointed.

"Well, we'll save it for later, then. After we've won. Maybe we can go somewhere to celebrate? Just the two of us?"

Lara hid her distaste. It wasn't just his appearance — over fifty, overweight, red faced and sweaty — but also the fact that he was married.

"We have to win first, Monty. Let's just focus on that."

"Okay, okay, whatever you say," he was still smiling, but he looked a bit crestfallen.

"Well then, Ms. Steele," he said, trying to sound upbeat, "shall we do this?"

"Let's do it, Monty," she replied and gave him her best smile.

The case was fairly simple - a small company had, in fact, been ripping off their products and selling them with a very similar logo. It was an open and shut case and small time, but Lara knew that it was a step on the ladder, albeit a small step on a long ladder. It was a way to introduce her to the client as a litigator and showed that the company had faith in her and saw her as a prospect for the future. She had been excited when she had been given the case. But that seemed like a long time ago. Now, she just wanted to get in there and get it done.

They all took their seats in the courtroom. Lara smiled at the litigator on the opposite side of the room. They knew one another and were on reasonably friendly terms.

The judge came in and the show began. Lara stood up, took a deep breath and began her opening argument.

"Your honor. This is a simple case and one which should never have gotten this far. It is quite clear that the defendant is in contravention of the following patents, as well as copyright law..."

As she plunged ahead, she got into the zone. She felt good. The case had taken a while to prepare, in order to get everything lined up and watertight, but she knew that it should all be over within a day. She thought it was slightly ridiculous that the other company had let things get this far, but maybe this was their first time in such a situation and they didn't know just what was coming their way. They were about to learn.

By the time they broke for lunch, Lara was confident that the whole thing would be wrapped up by the close of day, which suited her. As she left the courtroom, it surprised her to see Mr. Peters waiting. He was talking to Monty. When they saw her coming, Mr. Peters turned and smiled at her.

"Well, Lara. You have been getting rave reviews from Monty here."

Lara smiled.

"Great, I'm glad he's happy!"

"Very happy," Monty added, "It shouldn't go on too much longer now, should it?"

"No, I think it will be over today."

"Well, let's all go for lunch then, shall we?" Mr. Peters said, and they all headed to the court cafeteria to eat. The food was surprisingly good, but Lara thought about the years ahead that she would spend eating here and knew that she should try to find somewhere else nearby, just for a bit of variety.

Mr. Peters tried to frame his appearance at the court as an act of support, both for Lara and for the client, but Lara knew that she was being appraised. She wished that she hadn't seen Mr. Peters after all, that he had just slipped in at the back and watched her work.

When they returned to court, she felt the pressure on her. She faced the judge but was now all too aware of the eyes on her from the back of the court.

She stumbled over words, losing the thread of her argument. And the more she did so, the more frustrated she got with herself. At one point, she stopped.

"I'm sorry, I just have to check my notes for something," she said and returned to her table, her head down, pretending to read her notes when in fact trying to hide the tears in her eyes. She blinked them away. The angry tears would not escape. *This isn't fair! It shouldn't be like this,* she thought to herself. She did her best to compose herself and went back to work.

She managed to get through the rest of the day and the case was an easy win for her. But it should have been easier, and she knew that. She was frustrated and disappointed in herself.

She saw Mr. Peters and Monty deep in conversation outside afterward.

She headed over to them.

Monty was full of thanks and praise.

"Oh, well done, Ms. Steele! Well done!" he said, hugging her. She didn't even try to rebuff his advances at that point. She just felt tired. Tired of all of it.

After Monty left, sensing he wasn't going to be getting that celebratory dinner date he had been hoping for, Mr. Peters turned to Lara.

"Lara," he said, "shall we go for a coffee?"

"Of course," she knew that she had let herself down and she would just have to take whatever was coming her way now.

She turned in the toward the cafe, but Mr. Peters took hold of her arm.

"No, this way. I know a much better place just around the corner. The food here is acceptable, but the coffee leaves a lot to be desired."

Lara let herself be led away. At this point, she just felt worn out by everything… Craig, work, she just wanted to get into bed and leave it all behind.

They walked for about five minutes before they got to a small coffee shop. Lara could smell straight away that this was a place that took its coffee seriously. When they were inside, she recognized a few faces from courthouse. So, she thought to herself, this is a pretty well-known secret spot. I guess I'm being initiated.

They got their drinks and sat down. Lara shook her foot nervously, unsure what was coming next. Mr. Peters paused, gathering his thoughts, and then proceeded.

"So. What happened? This afternoon, I mean."

"I don't know, sir. I just... I lost my way a bit. My train of thought. I didn't sleep very well last night. I know that's no excuse. I'm sorry."

"Well, lucky for you, I actually snuck in early on and watched most of the morning session. I'm sorry if I put you off, but you must be ready for that kind of pressure. If you can't handle it when I'm there, then how are you going to cope when it's really high pressure?"

"I know, I know. I'm really sorry."

"Like I said, though, I saw you at work this morning and I was very impressed with what I saw. So, don't worry about it too much. But, I have to admit, you've seemed a bit... I don't know, frazzled, maybe... recently. There were moments this afternoon where you seemed to get quite emotional. I worried for a moment that you might have a full-blown meltdown. Can you imagine what it would be like if you fell apart in front of a grand jury? Can you imagine what some of those old dinosaurs back at the firm would say if they saw something like that?"

"I don't know what to say. It's not like me, it really isn't."

"I know it isn't, which is why we're having this conversation between the two of us rather than me reporting back to the board directly. Monty was thrilled, as well, so that's something else in your favor. I don't need anyone else needs to know about this. I know how it could damage your career, just as it's getting started."

"Thank you, sir. Thank you so much."

"But I think maybe you need a bit of time off."

"Sir, no, really. I'll be okay."

"No, look, it's not this big negative thing that you might think it is. This is just something we make all our junior associates do. We put them on a period of paperwork and legal research. You haven't done it yet, which is quite unusual, but it speaks volumes about our faith in you. We put you straight in at the deep end. But now, I don't want to undo all the outstanding work you've done, see you go back to square one. So, I think we'll slip you into the research role that you should have done at some point anyway, and then your career won't have to suffer. It will be good experience for you anyway, it will help make you more well-rounded in your role."

"Research? You mean, just going over papers, looking things up in books?"

"Well, there is more to it than that. It helps you to get a better understanding of the law and how things work. It's something everyone has to do. Honestly. And the great thing is that you can work remotely for quite a lot of it. So, if you feel like maybe you'd like to go and work somewhere else, maybe get out of the city, get a bit of fresh air, just reset a bit, it could be an ideal opportunity."

"This sounds like I'm being... I don't know... exiled or something."

"It's not like that at all. Really. If I didn't have faith in you, then we would be having a very different conversation. You have a whole career ahead of you that will be absolutely non-stop. In years to come, you'll look back on this little time away from the rat race as a very happy and restorative experience. I really believe that. In fact, I've seen it before. With other lawyers in the firm."

Lara felt close to tears, again, but she knew that she had to keep herself together.

"So, that's it then? I don't have any say in it?"

"You can have your say if you want, but it won't make any difference. This is just a natural, normal, part of your career path."

Reluctantly, Lara agreed. She would head to the office for the rest of the week to get assignments and briefings about what she would be doing, and then she was under no obligation to come in and could work from home.

"I really do suggest you take advantage of this time, though," Mr. Peters said kindly. "Get away from here. Take a step back. Then you'll be raring to go when you're all finished. Trust me."

Going home, Lara felt even more depressed. Work had gotten her through her tough breakups before. Now that was taken away from her. What was she meant to do with her days? Sit at home and stare at the walls? While doing monotonous paperwork alone with her thoughts? She couldn't do it. She just didn't know if she could cope with it, day after day.

But life sometimes has a way of intervening at just the right time.

CHAPTER 2

She returned home to her apartment. It was still light outside, but the light just bothered her now. Normally she would enjoy relaxing, watching the sunset. But she angrily pulled her curtains closed and sat there in the gloom.

"Don't you cry," she scolded herself, even as she felt her eyes welling up. What was she meant to do now? She told herself that moving forward started with that first small step. She told herself that she should stand up, take a shower, get changed, cook some food, do something. But she just couldn't bring herself to do it.

Her phone rang. She grabbed it. She knew that she was being too keen, hoping that it was Craig calling to let her know he had made a huge mistake. But, of course, it wasn't him. *He had probably moved on already,* she thought bitterly.

It was her best friend, Sienna. For a moment she considered rejecting the call. She wasn't sure if she could deal with anyone at that moment. But she knew that even if it was hard, it would ultimately be a positive thing to hear a friendly and familiar voice.

"Hey, Sienna," she answered the phone, trying to sound cheerful.

"Hey, babe, how are you?"

"I'm... I'm okay..." and then she began sobbing.

"Lara?" there was a note of genuine concern in Sienna's voice, "Are you okay? What is it? What's wrong?"

And then, between sobs, it all came out. As hard as it was to talk about, it was cathartic, as well. Sienna listened, first to the story of Craig, and then how it had negatively affected Lara at work that day.

When she had finished telling everything that had happened, Lara told her she knew she was just repeating negative patterns and expecting a different outcome, but that she didn't know how to break the cycle. This was where Sienna came up with her idea for turning things around.

"Do you remember last summer when I went on that trip?" she asked.

"Yes, off to Colorado or somewhere, wasn't it?"

"Wyoming. But yeah, same mountain range, I guess. Anyway, I had an amazing time there. It was more than just a holiday for me. It was a kind of reset. I don't want to say 'cleansing', I know how that sounds, like some kind of hippy mumbo jumbo, but that's what it was like. I just had all this nature around me, all this peace and quiet. It really allowed me to take a step back from things."

"Come on, you know me, Sienna. You know I'm a city girl at heart. I don't know if I could get into that sort of thing. Going back to nature, living off the land."

"Oh, it's not all like that. The cabins are well equipped. I wouldn't say luxurious, exactly, but they're comfortable and cozy enough. They have all the comforts of home, anyway, that's what I mean. Plus, a nice wood burner for the cold nights. You could be happy there. Just get away from things and have a bit of time to truly unwind."

"I don't know."

"Well, I really think that it would be perfect for you. And what's the worst that could happen? You go out there, you don't like it, you come home. Easy."

"I'll think about it. I promise."

After that they chatted for a while about other things, and Lara felt her spirits lifting. She was glad that Sienna had called her. If it wasn't for that phone call, she probably would have just stayed sitting there in the dark, wallowing in self-pity.

After she hung up, she showered, made herself a light snack and had an early night.

Although she felt better after their call, she had a restless night, waking up frequently and feeling the loneliness and anguish.

The next day, all thoughts of Sienna's idea were pushed to the back of her mind. When she arrived at the office, Mr. Peters took her to see one of the partners, who began briefing her on her new responsibilities. Straight away she hated the sound of it. It seemed like being locked up in some basement office in the building, poring over files, or doing the same thing but at home.

She got through the first day of it, but on the way home she felt her anger solidifying into determination. If she was in a situation she didn't like, then she'd do everything possible to make it better, to make the most of it. As soon as she got home, she looked up the cabins Sienna told her about. It was true; they looked far nicer than she had imagined them. In fact, they looked very cozy. She paused for a minute, arguing with herself, and then did it. *What the hell, what was the worst that could happen?*

She booked in for a month. She was told she could work

remotely for at least two months, so she could always extend her stay if she enjoyed it. She decided that no matter what, she would give the place two weeks. If she truly hated it after that, then she'd cut her losses and head home. Whatever happened, she decided that the break would do her good.

The following day she went into the office and told them she was taking the option of working remotely.

Mr. Peters came to see her in the afternoon.

"I hear you're going to be heading off," he said.

"Yes. I've taken your advice. Maybe I do need a bit of a change of scenery to make me appreciate what I've got."

"You'll come back a whole new woman, Lara. Trust me."

"We'll see."

And so it was that the following morning — having spent most of the previous evening agonizing over what she should and shouldn't pack, what would be suitable attire for the outdoors lifestyle — Lara loaded up her car and set off on the long drive to Wyoming. It was a two-day drive, so she would stop for the night in Omaha. That still left a long drive ahead of her the following day.

As she left the city, she kept looking in her rear-view mirror time and time again. Every time she looked back there, she saw it shrinking, shrinking, behind her. Her doubts grew. She felt slightly ridiculous. *What are you thinking? Cabins in the woods thousands of miles away? It's not too late,* she told herself. *You can go back home, veg out on the couch with some ice cream, and you'll be fine.*

But every time that voice started whispering in her head, she shut it off. To go backwards was to retreat. She had to push on. Had to keep moving forward. She locked her eyes on the road ahead and quit looking back.

Finally, she checked into a motel and ate a lonely dinner in a nearby diner before returning to her room. She had a moment where she was assailed by all her doubts once again, and she her face with her hands and cried. She wondered if she should just give up and turn around in the morning.

But when morning came, she felt better. She was far more determined. She got up at the crack of dawn, knowing that she had a long way still to go. She stood outside sipping coffee in the frosty air. The motel was on the edge of town and she could look away, across the plains. She was looking at land she had never seen before, at new beginnings, new horizons. She started to feel the first stirrings of excitement.

As the day progressed, she noticed the land getting more and more rugged. The wide-open plains of middle America gave way to forests and hills. In the distance, she could see mountains rising up that took her breath away. All of this within driving distance of her safe, warm apartment in Chicago - all the majesty of nature right there in front of her. It was incredible. The vastness of it all just hit her head on, and the sense of wonder didn't fade, it only increased the closer she got to it, the more immersed she became.

By evening, she reached a small town nestled in a deep valley between high hills, and even higher mountains behind. A river flowed past the quaint shops and houses that hugged its banks. A sign at the edge of town read "Sunset Ridge - Welcome to the Heart of the Mountains." She debated stopping at a gas station and getting a coffee, but decided she'd better push on. She knew from her online research that the cabins were still a ways out of town, up on a higher valley that reached deeper into the mountains to the north, and she was getting tired.

She reached the west end of town. Spotting a worn hand-painted sign that read "Mountain View Cabins," she took a right turn onto a gravel road that immediately climbed above Sunset Ridge.

The drive to the cabins took longer than she had thought it would. The mountain roads were difficult to navigate, and by the time she got to where she was going, the road had gotten narrower and narrower, until it was little more than a single track road. Trees closed in on all sides, forming a canopy over the track. She had left Sunset Ridge about fifteen miles back. Lara told herself that she would need to make sure that she kept some spare gas for the car handy, just in case. She started to have all these images of being stranded out there.

She checked her instructions. She had been told to follow this path until she came to a cabin with a light on. She continued cautiously, eventually spotting a place that fit the description. There was a pickup truck outside.

She pulled up, and the occupant must have heard her, as he came outside and walked over to greet her. She got out of her car. He was tall, a bit over six feet, at least, with broad shoulders. He looked as though he was in his sixties but looked good for his age. His face was creased and lined, but it looked worn by nature, rather than by age. He carried himself like a man twenty years younger — upright, with no sign of weariness. He was wearing a heavy plaid shirt and faded jeans.

"Evening," he said to her, extending his hand, which she shook. It felt rough and calloused, but gentle all the same, "You must be Ms. Steele."

"Lara, please."

"Pleased to make your acquaintance. My name's Clint. I'm the caretaker around here, so if you need anything while you're with us, please let me know straight away. Anyway, let's get you up to your cabin. You've still got a bit of a drive, but not too bad, and I think you'll agree that the views more than make up for it when you get up there. You just follow me, and we'll be there in no time."

And with that, he headed to his pickup.

He drove slowly on the track leading to the cabin. It was fairly steep and, while his pickup could no doubt handle it with ease, he knew her little car might struggle with it.

These were not driving conditions Lara was used to, anyway. It was a couple of miles further to the cabin where Lara would be staying. It was definitely remote. She pulled up next to Clint and climbed out of her car. Stopping to look around, she couldn't help but gasp. Trees surrounded them, but there were breaks that offered views down into the valley far below, through which a river roared. She could see the forest stretching out for miles, with the mountains rising in the distance, jagged and imposing.

She stood for a moment, lost in thought, staring at the deep forest in the distance. For some reason, she felt her eyes drawn to one otherwise unremarkable gap in the trees. She had forgotten everything else except for that view in front of her, and she almost jumped in shock when Clint coughed politely to get her attention.

"Yep, that view sure is something, eh?" he said, smiling. "Anyway, here's where you'll be staying."

Lara turned and had a look at the cabin, something else that she had all but forgotten about when she was hypnotized by the view.

It was small and looked pretty rustic. She did notice a satellite dish, however, and solar panels, so she wasn't going to be going completely back to basics, at least.

When they walked inside, however, she was pleasantly surprised. The cabin was larger than she would have thought - it stretched back further than she had realized from the outside. The open plan main area had an L-shaped sofa next to a wood-burning stove that sat in the middle of the room. There was a kitchen at the other end that looked quite modern, but still in keeping with the overall ambiance. She noticed that there was no TV, but she was quite happy about that. The floor was wood but covered with area and throw rugs.

"So, welcome to where you'll be staying. I stocked up the cupboards with some essentials — coffee, some pasta, sugar, that sort of thing. There's also some milk in the fridge and I made you a quiche as well, which I left in the fridge for you, I figured you probably wouldn't have eaten today."

"A quiche?" Lara couldn't help herself and laughed. "Sorry," she said. "It's just, well..."

"I know, I know. I don't look like the baking type. But I'm pretty good at it. I hope you enjoy it. Anyway, the bedroom is back there, and it's got an ensuite bathroom. I turned the hot water on this morning so you should be good to go, but if there's any problems just give me a call, okay?"

"That's great, thanks. Is there anything else that I need to know?"

"Well, I do have to give you my standard safety speech now. Obviously, this isn't the city like you're used to. I don't mean to sound patronizing or anything when I say that, but this is wild country. It is very easy to get lost. There's plenty of paths around here, even some old logging tracks. Stick to them, always keep in mind where you are, how long you've been walking for and make sure you know how to get back to the cabin when you need to. There's a compass here as well, so you should practice with that if you get the time. You're going to be here a while, so hopefully, you'll get around to it. It could save your life. You can see how vast this place is from the view out there. It's not to be taken lightly."

"Of course. I'll be careful."

"And at this time of year, the weather can be deceptive. It can lull you into a false sense of security. But it can turn at any point. Hell, I know it was warm today, but we could easily get snowfall in a few weeks. So, whenever you head out, always check the weather forecast, but also check the sky — that's the best indicator. And whatever you think, take extra clothes with you to keep warm, just in case. Best to be prepared, right?"

"Right."

"Then, there's the animals. Now, they mostly keep away from where people are, but every once in a while, one of them strays over this way. Normally they are far more scared of you than you are of them — even if it doesn't seem like that to you at the time — so if you see a bear or a cougar, just back away slowly, maintain eye contact, if you can, and you should be fine. And don't leave any food outside. Or even any garbage. It will attract them. I can come and collect it if you need me to, just call me."

"Okay, I should be fine with that, thanks."

"And finally. This is the bit where I don't want to scare you, but I have to make sure you are forewarned. There are men who live out in these hills. They're nothing to worry about, really. Most of them are just normal men, good men at heart, who just wanted to get away from society, or they're running from something out there. A lot of them have their own demons that they are fighting with, and there are a few who are... a bit touched. They're fine for the most part, but if you see any of them out there, don't engage them in conversation, just go about your business and let them go about theirs and you'll be fine. It's nothing to be worried about, as long as you treat them with respect."

"Right...okay. Wow...I wasn't expecting that!"

Lara's head was filled with visions of wild, half-naked men roaming the forests. She heard the wind pick up outside and shuddered slightly. Where were these men now? Where were they huddled, alone out there in the darkness? What were they thinking? What fires kept them warm, what thoughts drove them?

Clint saw her looking at the window.

"Ah, look now, I've spooked you. Honestly, they're none too close to you here anyway. I know where most of them have their stomping grounds, and I am sure you won't even see any of them. But just in case you do, just act natural, but act cautious all the same. Okay?"

"Naturally cautious. Gotcha."

He smiled and left her to settle in, leaving his card and reiterating that she should call him if she had any problems at all.

She grabbed her bags from her car and brought them inside. She closed the door and looked around. *Well,* she said to herself, *here I am. For better or worse.* She still had some misgivings, and she still felt out of place, but she hoped that would pass.

For a moment she felt overwhelmed, a wave of panic rising in her, and she was tempted to go stand outside and look at that view, breathe that fresh, crisp, mountain air until it passed, but she forced herself to be productive. She took her bags to the bedroom.

She hadn't had a look at it before, but it fit in well with the rest of the cabin. Wooden floors, a very large, old looking but comfortable bed, heavy wooden furniture. It wasn't massive, but it was big enough.

She put her bags on the bed and then went to check the bathroom. There was an old, deep cast iron bathtub with claw feet. She ran her fingers along the side of it. It looked like it would be a great place to begin unwinding.

She spent some time unpacking and getting the place in order, then she went to the kitchen and looked through the cupboards. As Clint had said, he had stocked it up pretty well. There was a bag of mixed nuts, which she took out and began eating absentmindedly as she continued her inspection. She opened the fridge and saw the quiche which brought a smile to her face, and then she found the Wi-Fi password — acting as a reminder that she did still have work to do. She'd been traveling for the past two days but would have to get right back into it the following morning.

She then stepped out onto the porch.

It was a different feeling now that she knew she was alone. A couple of miles might not be a huge distance in reality. She knew Clint wasn't far away at all, but she felt quite isolated all the same. A part of her liked it, but another part of her wasn't sure how to feel about it.

There was a rocking chair on the porch, and she sat there, just enjoying the view. She breathed deeply. She closed her eyes, just for a moment, and really listened. She had expected silence, at least compared to the city, but there were different sounds. She could hear nature all around her. The branches creaking in the wind, leaves rustling, birds singing. She thought she could hear water running somewhere behind the cabin. She decided that she would find the source of that one day.

She relaxed, rocking backwards and forwards in her chair, and felt at peace. Craig, the office, the courtroom, it all seemed far away from her in that moment.

With the sun setting and the temperature dropping, Lara decided that it was time to head inside. She went in, ate some of the quiche — which was delicious — and settled in on the sofa with one of the many books she had brought with her. She hadn't even connected to the Wi-Fi or checked her emails on her phone. She was still well aware that she would have to get back to it the following morning, but for now she was enjoying being disconnected for a while.

She ended up going to bed early. It had been a long day, after all, and she slept deeply and without a single dream that she could remember.

It was still dark when she woke up, so she checked the time. It was far earlier than she would normally get up for work, and she lay there for a few minutes wondering if she should try to go back to sleep. But she didn't feel very sleepy. She had gone to bed early. Perhaps this could be her new sleep routine while she was here, she thought. She didn't have to keep regular hours, after all.

She didn't have to commute to work, either. So she got up, got herself some breakfast while making a mental note of any supplies she needed to buy when she went shopping, possibly later that day, and set up her laptop at the kitchen table.

The work was as monotonous as she thought it would be, but as she got into it, she started to get an idea of the logic behind making her do it. This was the behind the scenes, boiler room work that won cases. She found herself making notes for herself as she went along, as well as making the notes needed for the case.

When she eventually stopped for lunch, she was pleasantly surprised to see that she had done pretty much a full day's work already. She decided to take the rest of the quiche with her and go for a hike. She could finish work that evening. *This could be a great routine to get into,* she thought. A bit of work, a bit of time outdoors, and she would be good as new in no time at all. At least, that was what she hoped for. As she sat at the table working, she found her thoughts turning to Craig and that familiar ache was there, still gnawing at her.

She decided that some fresh air would be just the thing to occupy herself. The day was warm and sunny as she stepped outside with her lunch in her backpack. She looked around and tried to decide which path to take. She chose the one directly behind the cabin.

It was uphill and by the time it flattened out she was sweating and short of breath. The sound of water that she had heard was louder now. She headed towards it and found a stream flowing down from the hill that stretched up higher and higher to a peak that she couldn't see. Where the land had flattened out, the stream formed a pool. There was a patch of grass by the stream, and she sat there to have her lunch. The sound of the stream calmed her, and she almost fell asleep after she finished eating.

But she managed to rouse herself and continue exploring the area, careful not to go too far as she was all too aware of Clint's warning about getting lost out there.

By the time she returned to the cabin, she was feeling tired out, but in a good way. She felt at peace. She checked the time. *Okay,* she thought to herself, *I can get to town and buy supplies and get back before dark, have some dinner, do some more work, read a book, and then go to bed. Perfect.* She thought that she could get used to this lifestyle, although she certainly couldn't envision herself giving up her city life on a permanent basis just yet. Maybe in forty years or so, but certainly not anytime soon. It was a nice change of pace for now, though.

She got in her car and headed back to Sunset Ridge. She

hadn't been able to get a proper look at it before, so she wanted to have a bit of a look around. Pulling into town, she stopped at a little park on the west end of town that stretched down to the river. Stepping out of the car, she decided that a little walk would be the best way to sightsee.

There was one long main street that was lined with business. Lara passed a few small shops on her way down the street — a pet store, a hardware store, a bookstore — as well as a diner that seemed to be the only place that was doing any business with about ten people sitting at tables. Lara decided that one day, perhaps over the weekend, she would have to come and try the food, maybe meet some of the locals. If she was at the cabin on her own for the entire time, it might make her go a bit loopy, she felt.

There was also a bar, but that was closed and shuttered at this time of day. Lara couldn't imagine it ever pulled in much business, but it was obviously busy enough to keep going at least.

The street was quiet for the most part. The few people she saw around didn't seem to pay too much attention to her, which she was glad for, as she had been worried that they would all focus on "the stranger."

Finally, she got to the other end of Main Street and found the grocery store. It was pretty small, but surprisingly well equipped. She picked out a few essentials that she was missing, then brought them up front. She was the only customer when she got to the checkout. There was a curvy, middle-aged woman with short dark hair and thick glasses working the checkout.

"Hey, honey," the lady said with a big smile.

"Hey," Lara replied.

"Not seen you around, you visiting?"

"Yes, I'm just staying at a cabin up the road a bit."

“Oh yeah? One of the places Clint looks after?”

“That’s right, yes.”

“Oh, he’s a sweetie, isn’t he?” She packed the groceries into a paper bag as she spoke, taking her time, moving at a pace that seemed glacial compared to the fast-paced city.

“He seems very nice, yes. I only arrived yesterday, but he showed me to the cabin.”

“It’s a great location, huh?”

“Sure seems that way, yeah. I’m loving it so far.”

“How long are you here for?” The woman took her credit card, taking an imprint - Lara was shocked to see they didn't even have a point-of-sale machine.

“A month to start with. Maybe more. We’ll see.”

“A month! Wow, that is quite some time to be up there. You on your own, huh? Well, if you get too lonely, you can always come to town, say hello. We’re pretty friendly round here. My name's Beth Turner.”

“Thank you. I appreciate that. I might just do that. My name's Lara. Lara Steele.”

Beth reached out a stocky hand to shake Lara's. “Just don’t be a stranger, Lara. It’s good to check in every few days, even if you just stop by to chat with Clint. It’s lovely up there, but you probably don’t want to isolate too much. There’s some folk who do just that, go a bit wild and live off the land, so to speak. But they all have their own reasons for that sort of thing…maybe running from a painful past, or who knows what other reason. I mean, they’re harmless enough, mostly. Just... you know. Odd.”

“Thanks, I’ll keep that in mind.”

Lara returned to her car feeling slightly troubled. This was the second time she’d been warned about these people living off the land. She wasn’t sure how to feel about it. People told her not to worry, but then they told her to be careful as well. *What a mixed message,* she thought.

That was her taste of civilization for now, so she headed off back to the cabin. The sun was setting by the time she returned. She put some wood in the wood-burner and sat outside watching the sunset as her dinner cooked in the oven and the fire warmed her little cabin. The sunset was stunning, and she didn't think she could ever become bored with the sight of it. Overall, she was feeling content and happy.

However, the days passed and by the end of the first week Lara was already questioning her decision.

CHAPTER 3

She found herself pacing the cabin at night, feeling as though she needed to be doing something, wanted to be doing something, but there was nothing that she actually could do. The nights passed restlessly, and in the days she would go for walks, but by the end of that first week, rather than finding them relaxing, she felt as though she was looking for something, waiting for something to happen.

She yearned more and more for the city she had left behind, and she considered leaving. She had tried, hadn't she? She had given this place a go. It just hadn't worked out. There was nothing that she could do about that. Lying in bed one night, wrestling with these thoughts, she came to the decision that she'd give it a couple more days. After that, maybe it would be time to return to the city and get back to her life.

Having made that choice, she fell into a comfortable asleep.

The next morning she awoke, poured herself a coffee, and wondered how she wanted to spend the day. Looking at the clear blue sky overhead, she decided to go for a real hike, one that took her a fair distance from the cabin. She had tested out the compass and felt she knew what she was doing with it. She had been getting more and more adventurous with her walks, but now she wanted to go for a full day's hike. She had looked at some old maps that she had found in a drawer and thought that she had a good idea of where she was going. There was a path that headed in that direction, and she had packed up all the supplies she thought she'd need.

She set off early. It was a clear day and there was still a slight chill in the air, although she knew it would warm up quickly. There was a light mist rising from the trees. She breathed in deeply. In that moment, she wondered if she was making the right decision. It was, after all, a truly beautiful place. Maybe she should give it more time? She just didn't know.

But as she got going, her mind cleared, and all doubts and concerns seemed to fade away. She felt at one with nature, at one with her surroundings. She breathed deep as she felt her legs work as the slope rose gently. It felt good. Better than a trip to the gym. More... *natural,* she thought to herself. It didn't just reinvigorate her body, it reinvigorated her soul. When she was out here, when things felt right, everything made sense. It was just those days when things didn't quite fit that were making her doubt things. When things just seemed a bit jarring, when she felt this kind of manic energy that made her feel as though she wasn't hiking but somehow trying to walk away from things, escape things.

On this day, however, everything felt good. Everything felt right. As she walked along, whenever she found herself in an open space, when the trees thinned out for a moment, she would turn her face up to the sun and feel it warm her, cleanse her, energize her.

Perhaps it was because she was in a world of her own that she didn't hear anyone coming. Perhaps it was because they were moving silently through the forest themselves and she wouldn't have heard them even if she had been listening for them.

Whatever the reason, she turned a corner in the path and found herself face to face with a man. She gasped involuntarily and jumped back slightly. Their eyes locked, and they both looked shocked. She felt slightly afraid, but then she saw kindness in his eyes. There was sadness there as well, mingled with it. It was a look that almost made her think of a startled animal — not one that would attack, but one that would run — or so she thought for a moment. Otherwise, if it hadn't been for the look in his eyes, then Lara might very well have turned and ran. Even so, the warnings of Clint and the Beth at the store rang in her head and she stood, frozen.

If it wasn't for those eyes of his, then he would have looked quite intimidating. He was tall and broad shouldered. His arms were muscled, and his body looked strong, as though it was used to hard toil. He was heavily tanned. His hair was brown but looked bleached by the sun with lighter flecks in it. It was short and was probably the smartest thing about his appearance. He had a short beard and wore a well-worn flannel shirt and faded jeans. He carried a backpack with him.

"Oh!" Lara cried out.

The man stood there, looking as though he didn't know what to say or do.

"Hello," he said eventually. His voice sounded hoarse, as though from lack of use.

Is this one of them? Lara thought to herself. *Is this one of the mountain men I've been told about?* And though he was an imposing figure, somehow, she wasn't afraid at all.

"Hi!" she said, "my name's Lara."

"I'm Chase," he replied, and they both stood there, awkward with one another, neither of them sure what they were supposed to do next.

"So, I'm just staying in a cabin back that way," Lara said, "I'm just out for a bit. Taking a bit of a break."

"Oh," he replied, not offering any more.

"And you?" she asked, "do you live out here?"

"Yes. I live around here," and he looked over her shoulder to the land that he called home. All the green land, stretching far away, this was the place that he knew, the land that was in his blood.

"Well, it was nice to meet you," Lara said.

"You too," Chase replied softly, and went to walk by her.

Lara had an internal debate for a moment or two and then called after him.

"Wait!"

He stopped.

"If you... I mean, if you're ever back along this path, if you see my cabin, drop by and say hi. I'll be there for at least a couple more weeks."

She didn't know why she'd done it. She still had the warnings about these men ringing in her ears. But there was something about this man. Something that seemed good but sad, somehow broken. That was the best way that she could describe it, but it still seemed somehow inadequate to her.

"Thank you," he said softly, almost too quietly to hear. Then he continued on his way.

Lara stood watching him disappear into the trees. She had a slightly troubled look on her face. They warned her that some of these men were running from their past, fighting their own demons. She wanted to know just what was pursuing this poor man.

As he left her sight, she turned and continued her walk. But she couldn't quite shake the look in his eyes. In her heart, though she did not know it just yet, she had already decided that she was going to stay for at least a bit longer, just in case he decided to come around and say hello.

She wanted to get to know him, though she couldn't quite say why.

CHAPTER 4

Chase walked away from the encounter, shaken. It had been so long since he had experienced any real human company, and he had felt compassion from this woman. For a moment, he felt the shell he had built around himself crack, but he knew that he couldn't allow that. He knew that it was for the best, for everyone, if he kept himself away from others.

Chase had just been out checking his traps. He did this daily — if any animal had been caught in them, he didn't want them to suffer if they hadn't been killed outright.

He had lived in the mountains since he had returned from North Carolina. In fact, he had grown up in the foothills of the Rocky Mountains in Wyoming, so it had been more like a homecoming, really.

He had grown up in this country and as soon as he returned, he knew he was meant to be here. He felt that maybe he should never have left, that a part of him maybe had never left, and now that he was back, he could try to be whole again.

He had left his hometown when his parents' ranch had failed, and his prospects had narrowed down to nothing. He had gone away, lost and confused, and joined the army. There, he found a sense of purpose, something that kept him going. His career had led him to the elite Green Berets in North Carolina, and that was where he had met the woman who would become his wife.

But when he returned from the army to make a life with her, there had been traumas that he had not dealt with. He tried to make a life for himself, in a suburban world that he did not know. He tried to be a good husband, a good father to his young son, but the memories of the things that he had experienced in the army kept recurring and the panic kept building, the sense that something was wrong within him.

He tried escaping the memories. He tried taking himself out to nature whenever he could, out to the wilds of North Carolina, out to the wide open spaces, the rugged places where he could be at peace, and it helped for a while, at least. But then he would return home and it would build, and build once more, and he thought that he would explode in some terrible way.

Then there was an incident where it all came to a head. He did his best to push that memory down, as far as it would go. The memory of that time when he frightened his wife, frightened his son, frightened himself with the possibility of what could have happened. That night he could never forget, yet didn't dare remember.

And so, his wife left. She told him to come back to her when he was whole again. But he didn't know how to be whole, and he didn't know if he could ever trust himself around the people he cared about again, in case he hurt them in some way…in case the demons rose to the surface again.

He returned to his hometown, but it had become a ghost town. He didn't know where the people had gone. He didn't know where his parents had gone. But he knew that it wouldn't have been his final destination, anyway. He knew that it could only have been a stopover. He looked about the old place one last time, and then drove until he arrived to the edge of the wilderness. Then he parked up his pick-up truck and walked away from it, knowing that he would never see it again. He kept walking and walking until he found a place that felt right to him.

He looked at the land and knew that he was home. He knew that he was in a place where he could start to heal himself, and where there was no risk of him hurting others while he did so. He sat there - before starting to build a shelter, before unpacking his supplies - and he just felt at peace. At last, he had found peace.

CHAPTER 5

After the encounter, Lara continued her hike but struggled to re-immerse herself in the experience. Her thoughts kept turning to that man, to Chase. *What's his story? He didn't look like the wild-eyed lunatic I've been expecting to encounter out there. He seemed calm, peaceful.*

Maybe she was just starved of human contact, she told herself. But then, she had gone for lunch at the diner in town the day before. She had seen Clint on her way back, for that matter. That had seemed like plenty of human contact to her at the time.

No, there was just something about him that made her want to dig deeper and find out more. Something about him made her want to reach out to him.

She returned to the cabin later in the day and when she finally stopped, the exhaustion truly kicking in. She had hiked for pretty much the entire day, after all, so it was no surprise that she was so tired, as well as suddenly feeling incredibly hungry.

She cooked herself a bowl of pasta, mixed some sauce in, and ate it quickly. She then ran herself a hot bath to ease away some of the aches and pains she knew would be accumulating from a full day of exercise like that.

She wasn't in the bath long before she realized that maybe it was a mistake. She found herself so relaxed that she was almost falling asleep. Before she could sink below the surface, she pulled herself out, dried off, and went to bed. She fell asleep almost as soon as her head hit the pillow and she slept deeply the whole night through.

In the morning, she woke up early as usual, and worked after breakfast. She was struggling to focus however, as her mind kept returning to her encounter with Chase the day before. *While I've been sleeping peacefully, where did he rest his head last night? Did he think about our encounter? What's his life like?* She kept mulling this over in her head.

By lunchtime she was pretty much ready to give up on work completely for the day. She decided to go for an afternoon hike to try and clear her head a bit.

It was another beautiful, sunny day. As always, Lara stood and took in the view. Despite any doubts that she had felt over the previous few days, she never tired of looking out across this wide-open expanse, gazing at the mountains away in the distance. But now she looked out at the trees and wondered to herself, *is Chase out there? Somewhere? What is he doing?*

She checked the horizon. There wasn't a cloud in the sky. *Perfect.* Nevertheless, she packed some extra clothes in her back-pack, just in case.

She began hiking behind her cabin until she got to a ridge-line at the top of the hill. The trees thinned out here and Lara had incredible views in all directions. She followed the ridge until it narrowed down to a thin path that dropped off on both sides. Luckily, she didn't suffer from vertigo, but she was feeling somewhat precarious, balanced there with a drop to her right that was becoming more and more sheer as she edged along.

She told herself to turn back, that she was stupid to continue, but she could see the peak just ahead of her, and was determined to make it. So, she pushed on. Every gust of wind that hit her caused her to freeze as she feared she would get blown off the side. She walked slightly crouched with her hands out for balance. She did her best to keep her eyes focused on the path ahead, the peak ahead, rather than the drop. *This is silly,* she told herself. But then another voice, a voice she recognized as the determined, strong voice she hadn't heard for far too long, told her, *go. Take one step at a time. You've got this.*

It was true. She did have it. Soon enough she was at the peak. She stood there, her heart pounding, her legs shaky, hands on hips just taking in the view.

Wow, she said to herself. She let out an almighty yell, throwing her head back and her arms out. That felt good, cathartic, somehow. She wanted to do it again. She looked around, wild-eyed, feeling alive. Then she threw her head back to let out another yell, but the yell turned to a cry of fear and surprise as the large rock beneath her feet suddenly shifted and the ground that seemed so solid just a few seconds ago completely disappeared. She felt a lurching feeling and a flash of fear as she plummeted down. She desperately failed her arms, trying to grab at something, anything... and then suddenly, with a painful wrench on her arm, she stopped.

She looked up and saw that her wrist had wedged between two rocks, thankfully only a few feet down from the ridge. She tried to pull herself up, but she couldn't find anything to grab a secure hold of. She tried to use her feet to help push herself up, but the rock wall beneath the ridge was nearly vertical and the rock itself was quite smooth. She couldn't get enough leverage to move upward.

Her sense of panic increased. She flailed her free arm up, desperately trying to find anything to grab onto, finding nothing. Her wrist began to hurt even worse as her arm began to go numb at the shoulder.

But then something grabbed her. It was a hand. A large, strong hand.

She heard a voice she thought she recognized, "I've got you. I've got you," it said, comfortingly.

She looked up and saw a bearded face peering over the edge of the cliff. It was Chase!

"Help me!" she cried.

"Stay still, don't panic," he said, although it was a bit too late to stop her panicking. But she stayed still as he pulled her. He was gripping a tree stump with his other hand to stop from getting pulled over himself as he lifted her up far enough for her to grab hold of the edge and pull herself up with his help.

She got over the edge and back to firm ground and stayed there, on her hands and knees, panting, overwhelmed.

Then she looked over at Chase.

"Thank you," she said, "thank you so much."

"Ah, you're welcome."

"How did you know I was here?"

"I was back down in the trees further down the hill. I saw you on the ridge-line. I know it can be pretty dangerous up here — it's quite loose rock, so it can roll away pretty easily. I thought I'd better come up and warn you before something happened. I guess I was a bit too late. Or just in time, depending on how you look at it."

"I'd say you were just in time. Thank you, so much. Gosh, I feel pretty stupid..."

"Not at all. How were you supposed to know?"

"Well, if I didn't know, then I should have been more careful. I just wanted to see the view."

"And the view sure is something, isn't it? Well, you're safe now, so why not take in the view? Just stay away from the edge."

They sat there together in silence while Lara calmed down. She could feel herself shaking, but it slowly died down. She looked over at Chase. He appeared to be completely calm, completely at peace with his surroundings. He sensed her looking at him and turned his head, smiling at her.

She hadn't seen him smile before. It was a kind smile, but there remained a look of faraway sadness in his eyes.

"Thank you again. You saved my life. Really."

"It's okay. Right place, right time."

"Please, at least let me cook you dinner or something to say thank you."

"You don't have to do that. Really."

"I'd like to, though."

"I'm not used to being around other people to tell you the truth. I don't know if I'd be good company."

"Well, let me be the judge of that. I'm not inviting you around just to entertain me, anyway. I want to say thank you. And it would be nice to have a bit of company. Wouldn't you like to have a bit of company as well?"

She wasn't sure if that was the wrong thing to say. She saw a look of longing flash across his face before he shielded it behind a mask of impassivity.

"I don't know. I'm kind of set in my own ways. Kind of used to my own company."

"OK, well, look. I'll make enough for both of us, and I'll serve it at eight tonight. If you're not there, then so be it. I'll have left-overs for the next day. No harm, no foul. Okay?"

"Okay," he sighed, sounding unconvinced.

"Great. That's settled then. Now, will you walk me back down the ridge just to make sure I don't have any further mishaps?"

He smiled again.

"Sure."

They walked back, carefully. They didn't speak much as Lara was concentrating on not slipping and having another near-death experience. One of those was quite enough excitement to last her for a long time.

When they did talk, Lara asked Chase questions about himself. But he seemed reluctant to answer, and it was hard to learn anything from him. Lara found herself answering her own questions more than getting answers for herself.

She told him she was from Chicago, that she was a lawyer. She told him she was working remotely at the moment. He asked her about herself, if she enjoyed the outdoor lifestyle, how she found the solitude.

"It's a nice change," she told him, "but it does seem a bit eerie sometimes, at night. See? This is why you'd be doing me a favor if you came by!"

She looked at him and saw him smile to himself and hoped for a moment that she was getting through to him. She thought that he seemed sweet, and she wanted to reach out to him. Despite outward appearances, there was something about him that seemed fragile and she wanted to help him but make sure she didn't do anything to scare him off.

"We'll see," he said. "Just don't be disappointed if I don't make it, okay?"

"I promise."

"Anyway, I have to go this way now. Are you going to be okay getting back on your own from here? You sure you know the way?"

"From here?" she looked around, recognizing landmarks and the path that led back to the cabin, "Yep. I'm all good from here. Thanks again."

"Okay. Just be careful of any cliffs getting back. Promise?"

"I promise."

There was an awkward moment, and then Lara did something that she hadn't planned to do. She reached out and hugged Chase.

There was a momentary pause, and she wasn't sure if she had done the wrong thing, but then he hugged her back. It felt good to her to have that human contact. She hoped that it felt good to him as well. She felt safe in his arms. And why shouldn't she? He had saved her, after all.

On the walk back to the cabin, her thoughts kept turning to Chase. She probably should have been thinking more about her brush with death and how lucky she had been to get away in one piece, but for some reason, it was him she couldn't get out of her mind.

When she got back to the cabin, she had a long, hot bath to help her unwind and wash off the dirt and grime of the day. Her wrist hurt where it had wedged between the rocks, and she had numerous cuts and scratches, but she didn't think anything was sprained or broken.

She had been planning to have a light dinner, but now she felt as though she wanted to make something more substantial, just in case Chase stopped by.

She checked the time and decided that she did, in fact, just about have time to make her favorite spaghetti Bolognese recipe. It involved a lot of simmering, but it was worth the effort. She had bought the ingredients planning to make the sauce one morning while she was working, but this seemed like a better time to make it. A good, hearty, home cooked meal would do wonders for Chase, she was sure of it. And maybe he'd relax and open up a bit.

She'd have to hurry though, to get that sauce simmering away on time.

So she went to work.

By the time she finished, the kitchen was looking pretty messy. She checked the clock. She still had time to tidy up a bit and get changed, which she did - removing her tomato splattered T-shirt and putting on something clean.

And then, she waited. By quarter past eight, she was feeling hungry. By half-past eight, she was going to give up. By quarter to nine, she decided to start plating up for herself, feeling somewhat disappointed as she did so, but telling herself that she had no right to feel like that. He had been up front with her all along, after all.

She breathed a deep sigh as she sat at the table, alone.

But then, there was a knock at the door. She jumped slightly, looking up, and then smiled. She hurried to the door and opened it, hoping she was right. And she was. There he was. He seemed to wear slightly more put-together clothes than before, and that touched her.

"Chase! Oh, I'm so glad you made it!" and she gave him another hug.

"I'm sorry I'm late. I wasn't sure about coming, so I kind of decided at the last minute. I hope dinner isn't ruined?"

"Oh no, not at all. I was running late anyway," she lied. It couldn't hurt.

"Come on, come in."

She led Chase in, and he looked about the cabin, taking it all in.

"Oh, this is very nice. Nicer than where I live, anyway."

"Where is that, if you don't mind me asking?"

"There's a few old hunters' shacks out there in the forest, if you know where to look. "Shack" probably makes it sound worse than it actually is. I've made it okay. Passable, anyway. It's enough for me, I guess."

"Well, make yourself at home here. Really, I mean it. Grab a seat and I'll make you up a plate."

Chase looked somewhat awkward in this new environment, and Lara was keen to put him at ease. He sat down at the table and Lara made him up a large plate of food.

"It smells amazing," he said as she was busy at the stove.

"Thanks, it's an old recipe of mine. It's nothing fancy, but it's reliable."

Chase took a couple of mouthfuls and then complimented her on how good it was. He spoke little for the next few minutes, however, as he demolished the plate full of food. It was the first proper meal he had eaten in a long time. Recently, all he had eaten was what he could catch and what he could grow. He had money to go to the town and get some supplies, but he just couldn't quite bring himself to do it somehow.

Lara watched him eating. She was curious about this man. There was so much that she didn't know — that she wanted to know. She was determined to get to the bottom of things.

He quickly finished his plate. She watched with amusement as he gently, almost daintily, dabbed with his napkin at the tomato sauce that was caught in his beard.

"Would you like some more?" she asked.

"Oh, no, really. I'm fine."

"No, I insist."

She made him up another loaded plate. And he demolished that one in a similar manner.

After he had finished, she dumped the plates in the sink.

"Please, let me do the washing up," she heard Chase say from behind her.

"Absolutely not. I'll get to it in the morning. Come on, let's go and sit on the couch."

They went through to the main living area and sat on the couch. Lara was hoping to learn more about Chase, but he was still reluctant to say much. She sensed that he wanted to open up, but somehow, he couldn't bring himself to do it. It was a frustrating experience as she sensed that there was so much below the surface.

"I do feel silly about today," she said after a while, "I mean, that was so careless of me."

"These things happen if you don't know the forests."

"I'd like to learn more if I could. Would you be willing to teach me?"

"I don't know."

"Please. It could help me out. Hell, it could save my life."

Chase sat, thinking about it. There was a part of him that didn't want to get dragged into someone else's life, that couldn't allow himself to become involved, but then there was another part of him that yearned for some kind of connection.

"Okay," he said. "I'll come and find you in a couple of days and I'll show you a few things. How does that sound?"

"Great! Oh, thank you so much! I truly appreciate it."

"You're welcome. Anyway, I'd better get going. I've got quite a walk back."

"But...but...it's still early! You don't have to go yet, do you?"

"I'd better."

He was already standing, and she knew that there was no point in arguing with him, so she simply stood to say goodbye to him. She had hoped to connect with him, but somehow it hadn't happened. But never mind. He had agreed to meet up again, and that was something, surely?

CHAPTER 6

Two days later, Lara was working away at her computer, contemplating what to do with her afternoon, when there was a knock at the door. She looked up and couldn't help but smile. She had been down to see Clint the day before, so she didn't think that it would be him. She had considered mentioning her meeting with Chase to him but had ultimately decided against it, although she wasn't quite sure why. Perhaps it was because of his warnings about the men who lived out there. She didn't want him to warn her off Chase and then have to explain that he was different, that he wasn't like those people Clint was talking about. She didn't want to have to justify herself to him.

So, she realized that it must be Chase at the door. She rushed to open it, and there he was, backpack on his back, still looking strangely awkward and unsure of himself.

"Hi, Chase!" she said, cheerily.

"Hi," he said. "Erm... I thought, I mean, you said to come around today, right?"

"Sure, yeah, come in!"

"Oh, I'm fine. I'll just wait here while you get ready, if that's okay."

"Sure, I just need to get changed quickly and grab some things. You make yourself comfortable."

He stayed on the porch, looking serene as he looked out over the land that stretched into the distance, looked at it as though it was his and he was a part of it, and as though it was a part of him. He looked as though he was in perfect harmony with his surroundings. Lara caught sight of him and she felt a sense of warmth towards him she couldn't quite explain.

She got ready as quickly as she could. She grabbed some food from the kitchen as well. She had eaten a large breakfast in anticipation of Chase's potential visit, just in case he came around before she stopped for lunch as he had, in fact, done. But all the same, she thought that it would be a good idea to take a few snacks with her to keep her going.

She bounded out of the front door. Chase stood up.

"So," she asked, "What's the plan?"

"Well, you wanted me to show you some things, right? I've been giving it some thought, trying to work out what I should show you, and I think the best way would be if we go for a hike and I just show you a few things along the way."

"Great! That sounds like a plan."

During the afternoon, all of Lara's doubts about staying out here in the wilds of Wyoming fully evaporated. Chase slowly and patiently showed her the country through his eyes, taught her how nature worked there, the balance that it created, how the entire system worked together, and she gained a whole new appreciation and understanding for where she was. She learned the magic of it and then learned that the magic was more than magic, because there was no trick to it. It was just the way of the land.

But it was more than just the land. She loved listening to him talk. She loved watching the quiet, gentle way he went about things, the almost shy way he went about revealing something, and how her delight in things gave him confidence and helped him to come out of his shell.

By the time they were finished for the day, Lara was as happy as she could remember being for a long time. For the first time since she had arrived in Wyoming, all thoughts of Craig and of her old life were banished.

She invited him to stay for dinner again, although she wasn't too sure what she could offer him, but he declined. She tried to insist, but she could see that he seemed tired, worn out by the day.

She realized that this had probably been more human contact than he had been used to for a while. She wanted to ask him more about himself, but every time she tried to broach the subject, he went quiet.

He made one comment about "when I was in Iraq," and she tried to pursue that.

"You were in Iraq?"

There was a pause. She looked at him and he looked away. She thought that he felt as though he had made a mistake, said too much.

"Yes," he replied quietly.

"You served there?"

"Yes," but she didn't have a follow up question to that as he didn't seem to be offering much.

She let him get on his way when they had finished for the day, sad to see him go all the same. He wanted to get back to his place before it got too dark, although she had every faith in his ability to find his way back in the dark.

She watched him retreat into the brush, having managed to make him promise that he would return soon.

"You mean it?" she'd insisted, "Because I really enjoyed today. And it was nice to have some company."

"Yes, I promise. I enjoyed it as well. It was nice to spend some time with someone and show them some of my world."

"Thank you for today."

That night, after dinner, she sat on the porch and looked across the land, peering, squinting, trying to see a light out there, wondering where he was and what he was doing. Also, she was wondering if he was thinking about her wherever he was.

In reality, she had not been far from his thoughts since he had left her. He had trudged back, barely even paying attention to his surroundings, going over the day's events again and again. It surprised him to find that he had enjoyed the day. He had not been sure what to expect, and he had been so nervous that he had almost not gone. But then he had thought about letting Lara down and he hadn't wanted to do that, so he had forced himself to overcome his nerves and go.

And he was glad that he had done so, or at least he thought he was. He still had some reservations. He liked Lara, he liked spending time with her. But he was cautious. He knew that he still wasn't quite right, he wasn't fully whole yet. He remembered how he had left North Carolina and he knew that he couldn't risk anything like that. He couldn't risk hurting anyone. He couldn't risk putting some poor unsuspecting person in the path of whatever it was inside him. That destructive thing that he couldn't quite contain.

He was so lost in his thoughts that he almost stepped into

something. He noticed it at the last moment and stopped himself and knelt to have a proper look at what it was. It was a wild animal dropping. He looked at it carefully, frowning slightly to himself. It looked like cougar to him. He hadn't seen any cougars around there, and it was slightly worrying that one had started to venture closer to him.

He told himself that he would have to warn Lara about that the next time he saw her.

He got back to his shelter, making sure he stayed alert the whole way back, ready to react if he saw any movement in the bushes. Luckily, there was none.

He sat by the fire outside his small hut, looking into the flames. He thought of Lara. He thought about just how good that human contact had felt to him. How natural. He had never appreciated just how much he missed it, how much he needed it. He saw her face in the flames, that smile, the way she nodded her head when he was explaining something or tilted it to one side when asking a question. But then the flames flickered, and he saw *her* face. He hadn't thought about her face for a while now. His wife. And in her face, he saw the face of his son... his boy. And he remembered everything that had happened. The emotion hit him hard. He felt a tear roll down his face. He tried to push the emotions down inside himself, although in reality it was something that it would do him good to face.

But for now, he couldn't do it. It was all too much for him. He tried to clear his mind and sat looking into the fire until it had burned low. Now, all that he could see were flames.

CHAPTER 7

Over the next couple of weeks, they settled into a routine. Every two or three days there would be a knock at Lara's door around lunchtime and they would head off on another adventure. Lara had quietly extended her lease on the place for another month and found herself getting up earlier every day to get her work completed quickly so she could go out exploring, using the new skills that Chase had been teaching her. She was learning the ways of the land. How everything worked in harmony together. She thought about her city life less and less. She knew she would have to return to the city soon enough. But she felt as though she was seeing the benefits of her time away. She felt more balanced, more at peace, more confident. Although her work was still important to her, she could see it as part of a larger whole.

Her walks took her further and further afield as she grew in confidence and learned the ways of the land that surrounded her.

One day when she was with Chase, she had what she felt was a breakthrough with him. He had been very guarded about his past and where he had come from, but he suddenly began to open up to her a bit.

They were hiking through the woods, enjoying the shade of the trees on a sultry afternoon, when Chase stopped.

"Away over in that direction, that's where I came from originally. Quite a few miles away, though."

"Do you ever go back?"

"No. I did, once, but there was nothing there anymore. Nothing for me, anyway."

"Oh," she didn't know what to say to that.

"Why did you leave in the first place?" she asked, eventually.

"Things had just changed for me there. I had to get out. So, I went away, joined the army, served abroad."

"Where did you go?"

"Afghanistan, Iraq. It could be hard. But we all just got through it in our own ways."

"How did you deal with it?"

"I don't know if I did deal with it properly. I did my best. I had a wife back home — back in North Carolina, that's where I'd go back to — and a son. That gave me something to focus on to help me get through things. But then when I left the army, I didn't deal with it all properly. I started to struggle with life in the suburbs."

"I can't really picture you in the suburbs. Washing your car, mowing the lawn."

Chase had looked troubled as he remembered his past, but he smiled slightly at that.

"I kept taking myself out into the wild — hiking, climbing, getting away from it all. It was only there that I could find any kind of peace. But I was kidding myself. It was a false kind of therapy, because as soon as I was back in the city, the memories would come back, the things I'd seen, and I'd be back where I started. No. Not where I started. It was slowly getting worse. In the end, my wife left me, had to take my boy away from me. I don't blame her. It was the right thing to do. For her, for him. Heck, probably for me as well, if I'm being honest. Then I was alone. And things were worse than ever before. The only thing I could think to do for myself to heal was to go back to the land I called home. So, I returned to my home town. But there was nothing there. It had always been run down, but it had gotten worse and it was just... empty. So, I headed off into the woods to find peace. And it seems to have worked."

"What happened with your wife? And your son? You don't have to talk about it if you don't want to."

"No, no, it's fine. Really. It probably helps to tell someone about it. I've been out here with my own thoughts this whole time. It feels kind of good to talk about it to someone, to be honest. I felt as though I was... kind of coming apart at the seams. It's hard to explain. I was struggling to hold myself together. And I guess in the end I couldn't. My wife thought it wasn't safe for her and, especially, my son to be around me anymore. I can't say she was wrong."

"Did you ever try to go back to them? To your family?"

"No. I just... I just can't trust myself. I don't know if it would be good for them to have me around, or good for me, either. I just don't know, and sometimes I think about it and I want to, but at the same time I get scared. Scared of what could happen."

They continued walking in silence. Lara didn't know what to say next, and Chase seemed to have exhausted his supply of words, at least for now. It was the most he had ever spoken to her about himself, and he had surprised himself. It had just seemed natural to him. He realized he was developing feelings for Lara, but told himself repeatedly that he couldn't do that, that it was dangerous for him to get involved, that he had to be alone. He had to protect her and protect himself. He didn't know if the demons would come back. He didn't know if they were completely defeated or just at rest.

As for Lara, his confessions had answered some questions for her but raised others. What had happened with his wife and son? Why had she felt unsafe? Lara always felt safe with him. She couldn't imagine a situation where she wouldn't.

They were both lost in their own thoughts as they continued hiking, until they came to some mushrooms that Chase wanted to tell her about, and then they easily slipped back into their old routine. But the thoughts remained.

It was a couple of days after that when Lara was out on her regular afternoon hike that she got the fright of her life.

She had gotten through her morning's work as quickly as she could, as she had spotted a trail that she was keen to explore. With her new found knowledge of the environment, as well as her newly acquired skills with a compass, she was confident enough to find her own way through the forest, while still staying aware that there was always the possibility of getting lost. She didn't fear the wild, not anymore, but she had certainly learned to respect it.

So, she found herself hiking up through the woods, working up a sweat and working off her lunch.

Every once in a while, she found her thoughts drifting to Chase and what he had told her about himself. She wanted to try and learn more about him, but at the same time she didn't want to intrude too much. She was still somewhat worried that she might scare him off in some way by prying too much. She knew that she had to be patient with him.

Every time her thoughts strayed, she tried to refocus on the path ahead, on her surroundings, tried to keep learning as well as enjoying the journey.

But perhaps her focus was still off and that's why she didn't hear the sounds in the trees. She didn't hear that something was out there, watching her, stalking her, coming for her.

She was starting to feel slightly worn out and decided that as soon as she found a good spot to sit down, she would rest for a minute and have a drink. With this thought in mind, she began looking for a suitable spot.

But then, she heard a rustling in the bushes behind her. It didn't sound like the wind. It sounded like something moving with purpose. She froze, feeling her heart beat faster. She told herself to remain calm and turned, slowly.

Back there, behind her, she saw two eyes glinting in the shade. The creature moved forward, slowly, and she saw something that filled her with fear. It was a cougar. Its eyes were on her, focused solely on her, as it continued coming on with slow determination.

She locked eyes with it and began walking backwards. She had been told by Chase that if she saw a predator she shouldn't turn her back on it, ever.

She tried to remember what else Chase had told her to do, but in her panicked state she kept drawing a blank. She remembered bits of what he had said. She raised her arms up to make herself as big as possible. Then she bared her teeth. She started to yell "Go! Go away!" she waved her arms at the cougar. It paused for a moment, unsure. But then it started coming on, again and again. She tried to maintain eye contact with it, but at the same time she was trying to look for some kind of weapon — rocks to throw, a branch to brandish — but she couldn't see anything that would help. Back, back, she went, but the cougar kept coming, closer and closer.

It darted closer and she yelled louder, waving her arms. It paused again, unsure. But it was closer, all the same. Then it came again. Lara's heart was pounding, but she fought the urge to run. She didn't know what she could do now though, as it moved in for the kill.

Suddenly, there was a commotion in the bush next to her. She turned and saw a blur of motion. Then Chase was there in the path, standing between her and the cougar. The cougar growled, raising a paw and beating at the air. Then Chase began yelling at it. He raised up the rifle he had slung over his shoulder, jabbing it threateningly in the air. The cougar paused, uncertain. It knew it was outnumbered now.

"Keep going backwards. Slowly," Chase said to her, sounding calm. Calmer than she felt anyway. The cougar growled softly. It took several steps closer, but Chase stood his ground, raising his voice again. The cougar stopped again. Then it turned and ran into the bushes. She couldn't believe it, couldn't tear her eyes away from the spot where it had disappeared, afraid that it would come back.

"Are you okay?" Chase asked, causing her to jump. She shot her eyes to him, her thoughts awhirl. Through the torrent of emotions rose one thought above the rest: *you saved my life. Again!*

"Yes. I'm fine," she managed, although she didn't feel like she was fine. "Oh my goodness…thank you, Chase." She began to feel her body shake.

"Thank me later. Right now, we need to get out of here. There's every chance that it's still out there, just getting its courage back. Come on."

He waited for her to get to him, then he took her hand and

began leading her away, back toward her cabin. They made their way quickly, but every once in a while, as though sensing something out there, Chase would stop and look back, searching the bushes for signs of the cougar. But luckily, it seemed to have truly disappeared.

Finally, they were in sight of the cabin. Lara could feel relief wash over her, but she knew they weren't out of the woods just yet — both literally and figuratively. She felt safe with Chase by her side, but she had to keep reminding herself that they weren't safe.

They finally reached the door to the cabin. She took her keys out of her pocket, but her hands were shaking, and she dropped them. She felt tears in her eyes, but Chase scooped down quickly and picked them up. He got the door open and then they were inside. Then they were safe.

Lara felt dizzy and felt herself wobble, then lose her balance. But Chase was there. He held her in his arms, pulled her close to him. He stroked her hair and whispered in her ear, "it's okay, it's okay," and she knew that it was.

She looked up at him, with tears still in her eyes.

"Thank you, thank you so much. You saved my life. Again!"

"Hey, it's nothing. Really. It's just luck that I was in the area."

Their eyes locked and they could feel the emotion, the tension in the air. They both knew something was about to happen, but they both feared it. However, it was inevitable. Lara leaned towards Chase and he bent his head down and they kissed. Immediately, they both felt the tension lift. They both felt as though everything had been leading to this moment. They both finally acknowledged to themselves what they really wanted. Lara reached up and ran her hand along his muscular arm. It felt good being held by him; it felt right. He had his hand on the back of her head, gently holding her.

But then he pulled away. She looked at him, smiling, but he looked unsure.

"I'm... I'm sorry," he said, "I shouldn't... I have to go."

Before she could answer, he moved quickly to the door, fumbling with the handle, and was gone. She ran to the door and called after him, "Chase! Chase, come back!" but it was too late. She slumped down in a chair, shaking once more. Her head was a whirl of thoughts she couldn't make sense of. The same was true for Chase, as he made his way through the undergrowth, head down, mind racing.

CHAPTER 8

Lara barely slept that night. She kept going over the events of the previous day. The cougar, Chase's rescue and then, the kiss. Ah, the kiss. She had wanted it more than she knew, until she was finally confronted with it. But now she was confused. She still didn't quite feel whole after everything that happened with Craig. She learned so much about herself out in Wyoming and she felt she was growing as a person, but there was a part of her that thought getting involved with another man — especially one as troubled as Chase — would be a mistake. She still needed time to become whole herself before moving on with someone else.

Chase barely slept either. He felt guilt at what he'd done, thinking he had taken advantage of Lara at a vulnerable time.

Lara spent the day watching and waiting, hoping to see Chase. By late afternoon, she had all but given up, when suddenly there was a knock at the door. She jumped up and rushed over to open it. It was Chase.

"Hi," he said, awkwardly, "can I come in?"

"Of course! Come on, I'll get you a coffee."

"No, no, that's okay. Thank you, though."

He sat down at the kitchen table with her. There was an awkward silence as they both waited for the other one to speak first.

Finally, Chase began to speak.

"Look, Lara. What happened yesterday... with you and me, the kiss I mean, that shouldn't have happened. It was just... it was just all the emotion of the moment. I do like you, Lara. I really do. But I can't do anything like that. I can't get involved with anyone. I'm still trying to deal with a lot of the things that happened to me. I still have my own demons to fight. I need to be alone."

Lara reached across the table and took his hand.

"It's okay, Chase, it's okay. Really. I do like you, but maybe it was just something that happened in the heat of the moment. I don't want us to ruin our friendship. Let's just pretend it didn't happen, okay?"

He looked at her with a look of relief and gratitude.

"Thank you," he said.

The atmosphere immediately relaxed and they began to talk more openly with one another.

This became the pattern they fell into after that. They would still go for their walks together, continuing their lessons on the nature of the land, but then Chase would also turn up unexpectedly for a cup of coffee and a chat. They ended up having deep conversations that lasted hours as they learned more and more about one another. One day, he explained to her more about what had happened with his wife, wanting her to understand why he was so cautious, why he was the way he was.

"One night, I woke in the middle of the night. I used to have these dreams, you see, bad dreams where I was back out there, amid... everything. It was as though I'd never really come back from war. I can't even remember if I was dreaming that night. But I woke up and I could hear someone in the house. I had a gun under the bed. My wife didn't know I had it. But I did. I wish I hadn't. I got to the door and opened it, raising the gun... and it was my son. It was my boy."

"Oh my...what happened?"

"Oh, nothing, nothing like you're thinking anyway. I didn't shoot him. But I had aimed a loaded gun at my son. It was unforgivable."

"You couldn't have known though, you thought that you were doing the right thing."

"But I wasn't. I was doing the wrong thing."

"You can't keep blaming yourself. It doesn't help."

"There's a part of me that knows that's true, but then there's another part of me that just can't quite forgive myself. Not yet, anyway. Hopefully one day. But I have to do it on my own."

"I understand. You have to find a way through it."

"I'm trying. I really am."

Lara felt as though it was the last piece of the puzzle. She finally understood exactly why he had to be alone, what he was working through. She was glad he had shared it with her.

As he left that day, they both saw a pickup truck pull up. It was Clint. He sat watching Chase. Chase looked at him and then hurried off in the opposite direction. Lara watched him go and then turned to Clint.

"Hello, Clint," she said as he exited the car, "how are you?"

"Fine, fine," he said, but he was looking in the direction Chase had gone.

"What did he want?" he asked.

"Oh, he's just been popping around a bit. Helping me with things."

"Hmm. Well, you know I warned you about those men who live out there in the wild. How you have to be careful around them. He's one of them. I know little about that one, but he seems to have his own problems. You be careful, that's all I'm saying."

"I will. I promise."

Lara didn't agree with Clint's feelings towards Chase, but she decided it wasn't worth arguing.

A couple of weeks after that, Lara woke up to find a note slipped under her front door. It was from Chase.

Lara, I have to go away for a couple of days to inspect some traps that I haven't checked in a while. I'll be back soon, I promise. Look after yourself and stay away from any cougars!

Lara felt slightly disappointed, but she was touched that he thought to let her know.

She stepped outside to see how the day was looking, and she was slightly dismayed to see that the skies were a dark gray. The temperature had also dropped significantly. She remembered Clint's warnings about early snowfalls and wondered if that was what they were in for. She hoped that Chase would be okay wherever he was, but there wasn't much she could do about it.

She went back into the warmth and got on with her work for the day. It wasn't until she stopped for lunch that she checked outside again, and she stood in the doorway shocked at what she was seeing. The entire countryside around her had turned white, covered with snow. She hadn't even realized that it had started falling. Her thoughts turned to Chase again, out there somewhere in this weather. She worried about him, but then she reminded herself that he knew what he was doing. He could live off the land and he would know exactly what to do in a situation like this.

Yet, the snow kept falling. By evening, her car was buried.

She'd seen nothing like this before. Chicago got some pretty extreme weather, but it had never snowed her in like this. She had never seen the snow pile up this quickly. She thought about the supplies she had. Would she be okay? She checked her cupboards. Things were running low. But she didn't panic, not yet. She knew Clint was down the road and that he would probably be up to check on her soon enough, seeing how bad the weather was.

So, she lit her stove to keep the cabin warm, and waited.

The following day, the snow had not let up. She couldn't believe just how much snow had piled up outside the cabin. There was a snow shovel in a cupboard in the kitchen, and she took that out and cleared a small area outside her door. The porch was covered and still relatively snow free, but she wanted to see how hard it was to clear the snow in the front driveway. She gave up pretty quickly. The snow wasn't as wet and heavy as back home along Lake Michigan, but there was a shocking amount of it. It was hard work to clear the porch, and the snow just kept piling up where she had cleared it. She headed back inside to warm up. She cooked a small meal for herself as she started to wonder when she would be able to get fresh supplies, and just where Clint was.

In fact, Clint had been keeping an eye on the weather and was concerned with what he was seeing. The other cabins were empty at this time of year, so his thoughts turned to Lara. By the afternoon of the second day, when the snow still hadn't let up, he loaded up his pickup with supplies as well as snow clearing equipment and got in to drive up to her. He knew it would be a difficult drive, but he had every faith in his old pickup. It had never let him down yet.

He headed out, giving himself plenty of time to get there before the last light of the day faded. But it was slow going.

He kept pushing on forward, through the snow. The road narrowed and he slowed down, making sure he kept the pickup under control. The light was starting to go, and he was struggling to stay on the track. It was hard work, but he thought he had things under control.

As he reached what he thought was the final corner, he turned the wheel as slowly and carefully as he could. But the pick-up truck kept sliding in the direction it had been going. Clint panicked as he saw the edge of the road coming closer and closer.

But nothing he could do made the slightest bit of difference. At the last moment, he flung open the door, ready to leap out into the snow. His seatbelt was jammed. He wrestled with it, but it was no use.

The pick-up rolled right to the edge. It balanced for just a moment, and then began to tip over. It was slow. Clint managed to finally unbuckle his seatbelt. He went to leap out of the door, but it was just a moment too late. The truck began to tip, speeding up. It began to roll over and over. Clint struggled to hold on, but he was slammed against the ceiling of the truck, and then it came to a stop, killing him instantly.

Lara, completely unaware of what was happening, continued waiting.

By the following day, there was still no sign of anyone. She couldn't get any phone signal and the internet had stopped working. She was completely isolated. The power also kept cutting out. Every time it did so, it filled her with fear, leaving her feeling even more isolated and cut off from civilization.

She didn't know what to do next. She was sure that whatever choice she made, it could end up being the wrong one. But she had to do something, and the longer she put it off, the more the snow fell, and the harder it would be to make that decision.

So it was that she set off into the snow. She had to search for help. She could no longer wait for Clint, or wait for Chase. After all, she had no idea where he might be. It was down to her to make her own way out of this. The snow had stopped falling and the clouds had cleared briefly, so she took this opportunity to begin making her way through the snow, desperately trying to get to Clint's cabin. She set off down the hill. She had wrapped herself up in her warmest clothes, but she still felt the cold, and she hurried as fast as she dared, while still stopping to check the direction she was heading in.

However, the snowfall was enough to confuse Lara. As the clouds rolled back in and she looked up at the sky nervously, waiting for the snow to begin again, she was already hopelessly lost. She just didn't realize it.

She kept going, trudging through the snow. She began to doubt herself, doubt the direction she was going in.

At last, feeling exhausted, she spotted something that gave her hope. She saw some smoke rising in the distance. That must be Clint's cabin, she told herself. Her strength renewed, she kept going.

As she drew closer, she began to have second thoughts. This wasn't Clint's cabin. It was small and looked run down. But it was something, at least. Whoever it was that lived there would be able to help her, she was sure of it.

She got there as quickly as she could, never taking her eyes off it.

When she got there, she knocked on the door. She heard a sound inside and then the door creaked open, slowly. A face peered out cautiously from the dark.

The man looked old, although it was hard to tell exactly how old he was. He had gray hair, wild and unkempt, and a long, messy beard. He looked at Lara without saying a word.

"Hello?" Lara said. "Can you help me, please? I think I'm lost."

"That you are," the man croaked. "Ain't nothing for anyone out here."

"Please help me," she begged. He paused for a moment and she thought he was going to close the door on her.

But then he slowly opened the door all the way.

"Come on, then," he said.

She stepped inside, grateful. The only light came from a fire in the corner. She tried to make out the interior of the cabin. The floor appeared to be packed-down dirt. There was a mattress in the corner. She couldn't make out much else. She didn't like it, but she had little choice.

"Thank you," she said. The man didn't reply. He squatted in the corner, glaring at her. The light of the fire danced off his face and Lara worried about the situation she had gotten herself into. She thought she saw the light of madness in the man's sunken eyes.

"So, do you live here, then?" she asked.

There was a long pause, and she thought that maybe he would not answer her. But then he nodded slowly.

"Yep," he croaked in that unnatural voice of his. "Lived here for a few years now. Best place to be. End times coming, see?"

"End times?"

"End times. The judgment. There's a reckoning coming, that's for sure."

"What kind of reckoning?"

"The evil will be judged, the world ended and born anew."

"Who are the evil?"

He nodded at the door.

"Them. Out there. All of them," and his eyes narrowed as he looked at her with suspicion, "Come to think of it, you come from out there. You one of them?"

"One of who?"

"One of the wicked. One of the damned."

"No, sir. I'm not."

"Liar!" he roared at her. She backed towards the door, as scared as she had been when faced with the cougar but once again trying to stay calm.

"I'm not lying."

She was at the door now. She didn't know where she would go, but she knew that she had to get out of there. She knew she was in danger if she stayed there.

She reached behind herself and tried to find the doorknob.

But it was too late. The man was rushing at her. She turned and tried to pull the door open, but she felt the weight of him against her. He pulled her and threw her to the ground.

"No, please," she whimpered as he stood over her, leering at her.

"No good trying to run," he said to her.

She tried backing away, but she knew there was no escape.

Just as he reached down to grab her, however, there was a crashing noise back in the corner of the cabin. The door had been knocked off its hinges.

And there, silhouetted against the daylight, she could see the shape of a man. He stepped into the cabin and she couldn't believe what she was seeing. It was Chase, standing like an apparition, like a dream conjured from her panicked mind.

"Get away from her," he said, his voice taking on a menacing tone that Lara had never heard before.

The man turned to him.

"You! What do you want?"

"I want you to let the lady go, that's all. Then you can get on with your day and we can get on with ours."

"Not going to happen."

They stood, staring at one another for a moment, the tension mounting. But then, when things happened, they happened fast. The older man lunged at Chase, letting out a horrid cry. Chase was a Green Beret, a Special Forces veteran, but the old man seemed to know what he was doing. As the two men struggled, Lara dimly remembered Clint's words that there were many vets living in the woods. Other men like Chase, wounded, deadly, capable, and suddenly she worried.

The man grabbed a hammer from beside the door and struck down at Chase, but Chase deflected the blow. He drove a hard elbow into the man's nose, drawing a grunt of pain, but the man kept going, trying to drive his forehead down into Chase's face.

Chase was able to get leverage with his legs and kicked the old man off of him. In a flash, Chase was on top, holding the man down, and suddenly the fight seemed to leave the old fellow.

"Alright... alright, you fool. I'll stop," the man grunted thickly through his broken nose.

Chase looked down at him for a moment, then stood up and turned to Lara.

"Are you okay?" he asked her. Despite the furious fighting, his breathing was hardly any heavier than normal.

She was about to answer yes, when she saw movement on the floor and cried out a warning to him. The old man, still shockingly quick, had grabbed a rifle that was leaning against the wall. Chase was on him again, struggling to gain control of the weapon. Lara couldn't see clearly what was going on and her heart was beating so fast in her chest she thought it would burst. Then, a powerful BANG, and she screamed. The gun had gone off, impossibly loud in the small cabin. There was smoke in the room and it was hard for her to make out what had happened.

"Chase?" she cried out.

"I'm okay, I'm okay," she heard him panting in the dim room.

"Is he?" she asked.

"He's dead. The gun got him. Don't look. You don't need to see this."

He came over to her and put a protective arm around her.

"Come on," and he led her outside. The clouds had cleared again and the storm she had feared returning looked as though it had passed.

"How did you know where I was?" she asked.

"I came back and wanted to check on you. I found the cabin empty, so I followed your tracks. When I saw you'd come this way, I knew you could be in trouble. I know little about this guy, but I've come across him a few times. He was never right in the head. There's some out here like that. But it's okay now. I'm here."

"Thank you. You've saved me again."

"It's okay, Lara. I probably should have come back as soon as the snow started. Anyway, let's get you back to my place."

"Why don't we just go back to mine?"

"Mine is closer. We can sit this out, then head to yours in the morning."

"Okay. What about him? We can't just leave him like this." Despite her fear, she suddenly felt sorely for the tortured old soul.

Chase stopped and looked back at the cabin, then looked up

at the sky. "We'll come back when the snow stops, I promise. Right now, we need to look after ourselves."

"Okay. If you say so. I trust you."

They began trudging through the snow. Lara tried to look back at the cabin they had just left, but Chase kept telling her to keep looking ahead.

Soon, the clouds had returned, and Lara worried it was going to snow again.

"How much further is it?" she asked.

"Not too far now. Looks like more snow is coming, we'd better hurry. I know a shortcut we can take."

He led her down through some bushes. They reached a wide and rushing stream - one that likely fed the river below the cabin, she thought to herself.

"Will we be able to cross this? It looks pretty dangerous."

"We'll be fine. Just don't slip on the rocks. Look, I'll show you the way."

Chase made his way across, jumping from stone to stone easily. Lara watched him carefully, but she was still nervous.

"Come on," Chase said, "you'll be fine."

She started making her way across. Just as she was almost there, she lost her balance. Her arms were flailing as she was about to fall backwards into the freezing water. Suddenly, she felt Chase's hand grab her firmly around the wrist. He pulled her, and she collapsed to the bank. But Chase had overbalanced himself with the effort, and he fell forward into the water.

He was up immediately and got himself out of the water, but he was soaked through and shivering already.

Then, as if things couldn't get any worse for them, it began to snow.

"We need to get you back as quickly as possible," Lara said, concerned.

"Let's go," Chase replied, his teeth chattering.

They hurried forward as the snow was falling again. It was getting dark. Suddenly, Chase stumbled and fell.

"Chase!" Lara cried out.

"I can't... I can't..." he muttered.

She looked around desperately. She knew that hypothermia was quickly setting in, and she had to do something about it right away.

"How much further is it?" she asked, but he just shook his head.

She tried to think what to do. She remembered some things she had read, and some of the things Chase had taught her. She remembered Chase mentioning how to build a shelter at the base of a large tree, where the thick branches kept the snow from accumulating. These clearings were called "tree wells", and were dangerous to skiers, but they gave excellent shelter from the wind and snow.

She looked around and, finding a perfect tree, began digging her way into the tree well. The snow had piled thickly in the storm, so it took some work, but before too long she'd made a hole large enough to crawl through. She guided Chase in, then began gathering as much wood from under the snow as she could.

Thankfully, the base of the pine hid several pieces of relatively dry wood and broken branches that would serve as kindling. She picked out the driest pieces she could find and formed a small fire. She piled the base with dead moss and took out some matches that Chase had told her to always carry with her.

Chase was still shivering as Lara tried to light the fire. It took her a few attempts and she began to worry her matches were going to run out, but finally, she got it going.

"Come on," she said to Chase. "Get close to it. You need to get warm."

Thankfully, he was still shivering. When he stopped, she knew it would be too late.

"You need to get out of these wet clothes, as well. You need as much heat as possible."

She helped him get out of his clothes. She couldn't help but notice how sculpted his body looked, but she didn't allow herself to become distracted from the task at hand.

He sat by the fire. She remembered reading about sharing body heat in situations like this. She felt awkward about doing it, but she reminded herself of all the things Chase had done for her and the fact that he had gotten himself into this dangerous situation by helping her.

So, as the fire continued burning, she began to strip down to her underwear.

Chase, still shivering, looked at her.

"What are you doing?"

"We need to share our body heat. You're still too cold. We need to heat you up fast."

He didn't respond, just looked away to save her modesty, although she was past caring about that. All she wanted was to help Chase.

She piled her clothes on the ground. She had already moved Chase's close to the fire to dry them out. The snow had started falling heavily, so she knew they were going to be there for a while, anyway.

She moved over to him, feeling slightly shy. She put her arms around him. He felt cold, so cold. She held on to him as he sat by the fire.

Slowly, she felt his temperature rise. Slowly, his shivering stopped. She kept her eyes on the fire, making sure it still had plenty of fuel.

"Thank you," he said after a while.

"You're more than welcome," she said, still holding him tight. He probably didn't need her heat so much now, but all the same, she couldn't seem to let him go. She rested her head on his shoulder. "After everything you've done for me, this is the least I could do."

He turned his head slightly until he was facing her. Before she knew what she was doing, she had kissed him gently on the lips. They felt warm. She leaned back to see if she had done the wrong thing. But he was smiling. He leaned in and kissed her in return.

The fire was blazing now, matching the fire that burned in their blood for each other. He moved over to her, closer. But he was still weak. She saw him waver slightly, then he stumbled.

"Chase, are you okay?" she asked, concerned.

He lay there, his breathing slightly labored, and looked at her.

"I will be. Just need a moment."

But she didn't want to wait a moment. Not a single moment more. They had already waited long enough, as far as she was concerned. She gently pushed him back, and he pulled her to him, wrapping himself around her. Outside their circle of light and heat, their movements of love were silhouetted by the roaring fire against the darkness and falling snow outside.

Later that night, Chase found himself just looking up at Lara, this wonderful and amazing woman, taking in the smell of her perfume and the sight and feel of her against him. He had been through so much, and had been alone for so long, that he just wanted to hold her to him. A flood of emotion swept through him, and he gently pushed himself up from her, turning his head so she wouldn't see the tears that streamed down his face, and then rolled over to lay behind her. He wrapped his arms around her, pulling her close, making her feel safe, and wonderfully drowsy. She stroked his arm, realizing to herself just how good it felt to be lying there with him wrapped around her. He kissed her lightly on the shoulder as she drifted off to sleep.

When she woke, the sky was starting to lighten and the fire was dying out. She reached over and grabbed some branches to throw on it.

"Hey," she heard Chase's voice behind her.

"Hey," she said, still sleepy.

"We should probably get going soon. The snow has stopped for now, but I think it could be back anytime."

"Okay. How are you feeling?" she asked.

"Fine. Great, in fact."

"Mmm. Me too."

She stroked his arm again.

"Come on," he said, "as much as I would love to stay here, we do need to get moving."

"Okay." They both stood up and got dressed.

"It's not far, now," Chase said.

They made their way to his cabin and arrived just as the snow started falling again.

His cabin was small but in much better shape than the one that Lara had been in the previous day.

Inside, it was comfortable and well furnished. There was a lot more room inside than it seemed from the outside. The furniture was all made by hand, but it was in good condition. Lara sat on the bed while Chase lit the fire.

When he had it going, he came over to the bed and sat beside her. He cupped her face in his hands and kissed her. It was just as wonderful as it had been the night before. Slowly they undressed one another and climbed under the covers, warm and happy to be together.

CHAPTER 9

The storm raged for about five more days. Lara didn't care by this point. They spent most of their time in bed. When they were not making love to one another they would just lay there, holding on tightly to one another, and speaking softly, revealing more about themselves. Lara told him about her career, about the troubles that had driven her to come out here. She also told him she had found the balance she needed.

Chase opened up to her about the things he had seen and done while at war. The things he had brought back with him in his mind. Things he had told no one before, things that had haunted him, stalked him in his dreams. And as he went on, and she listened to him, it amazed him to discover that by talking about it, he was exorcising some of the demons. He felt refreshed, renewed. He could still feel the darkness within, but it was lessened somehow.

The days wore on and the storm eventually ended. One day, they awoke to the sound of dripping water as the snow began to melt.

Chase stepped outside, squinting in the sunlight. He stretched and looked around.

"Well, I think maybe we should get you back to your cabin. Old Clint is probably going out of his mind wondering where you are."

"I know, I know. I just don't really want to leave."

"It would be lovely, wouldn't it? To just stay here forever."

"But reality has come knocking, I guess."

"I guess it has."

They began the walk back to Lara's cabin. It took most of the day, trudging through the deep snow. Chase went first, breaking the trail. It must have been hard work, but he didn't complain.

Finally, they got back to the cabin. They went inside and Lara brewed some coffee.

Chase sat at the kitchen table watching her.

She didn't speak for a while, and he could tell something was troubling her. Eventually, Chase spoke.

"You're leaving, aren't you?" he asked.

She stopped. She hesitated to face him, but finally she did.

"I have to," she said, "I just feel like it's time."

"I know. I understand."

"But why don't you come with me? We could make a life together in the city."

"I can't. I'm sorry, Lara. I would love to be with you, but I tried the city life before and it didn't work for me. I belong out here. I feel as though I'm finally beginning to get a hold of my inner nightmares, but I still don't trust myself in an environment like that."

"I thought you might say that," she said softly.

"I'm sorry."

"I know. And I understand. I do. I wish there were some way

that we could stay in contact though. I don't know how we could do it. But I just wish that we could."

"We'll work something out. Maybe Clint can help."

"It's worth a try, I guess."

They sat in silence, each lost in their own thoughts. They were shaken out of their private reveries by a knock at the door. Lara went to answer it. It was a state trooper. Immediately she looked at Chase, anxious, thinking that they had found the body.

It turned out that the trooper wanted to speak to her about Clint. The wreck of his truck had been found the previous day, but no one had been able to get up to Lara. She asked the trooper if there was anything she could do for Clint's family, but the man told her that Clint was a widower, without any children or grandchildren left behind to miss him. The thought left her feeling deeply saddened, remembering Clint's gruff but kind manner, and his surprisingly wonderful home cooking.

It also dawned on Lara that she should be proactive and tell the state trooper about the old man that had attacked her. She knew it was a chance to take - that the trooper could arrest her and Chase on the spot - but it would be worse if the man was discovered and they'd said nothing.

In the end, the troopers investigated and quickly came to the conclusion that Lara had been telling the truth. The man was known in the area, if not by name then by reputation as a dangerous person, and Lara's standing as a highly respected lawyer helped alleviate suspicions. Ultimately, the decision was made to bury the man outside of his cabin, in the place that had seemed to give his tortured mind some semblance of peace. Chase offered to help, and to say some words to a fellow wounded soul.

To Lara, the death of Clint and the investigation into the old man also made one thing clear - it was time for her to go back to Chicago.

It took a couple of days to arrange everything. The company who ran the cabins sent a representative up to make sure Lara was okay. Chase was still there when he arrived. As the man and Chase were talking, a sudden idea struck Lara, and she pulled the man aside.

"You need a new caretaker," she said to the man pragmatically.

He reached out his hand, a small grin on his face. "Alan," he said in greeting.

Lara shook his hand firmly, but quickly. "Alan," she started again, "you need another caretaker. Chase is your guy."

Alan gave her a quizzical look, then eyed Chase. Chase looked like he was trying to keep busy, without really knowing what to do with himself. "Him? But he's a wild fellow... Clint told me all about these guys. How can I rely on someone like that?"

Lara shook her head. "He's not like that, he's hurting. He's a veteran of Afghanistan and Iraq, and a Green Beret to boot. He needs some direction in his life, and this would be perfect for him."

Alan merely looked at her dubiously.

"I'm serious. You will not find a more capable person than him to take care of things and watch out for the tourists. He saved my life."

"Really?" Alan said, surprised.

"Yes... and not once. Three times, although I'm embarrassed to admit that, so let's just keep it to ourselves. Honestly, Alan. I'm a lawyer, I know how to read people. Give him a chance."

"Well..." Alan seemed to hesitate, but Lara was good at being persuasive. That's how she excelled in her career, being able to get others to see her side.

"Okay, I'll talk to him," Alan finally agreed. Lara gave a quick fist-pump, then looked at Chase and composed herself.

Alan turned and approached Chase. The two men began talking, and Lara left them in peace, busying herself with making everyone some coffee. She was confident Chase would see the opportunity for what it was and take the chance. Sure enough, when Alan was finished, he offered Chase the job of caretaker. Chase seemed unsure, but Lara gave him an encouraging look and he smiled and nodded slightly.

By the end of the afternoon, he had shaken hands with the man and they had agreed on terms. This was an enormous step for Chase. Finally, he felt ready to return to living among people, if only in his own small way. It was perfect for him.

At last, the day came for Lara to leave. There were more than a few tears as she said goodbye to Chase, but they promised that they would stay in contact with one another and they would try to make things work, somehow. She wanted to come back and visit him, even if he couldn't bring himself to join her in Chicago. They didn't know what the future held for them, but they both felt positive.

Chase was returning to the world, and Lara was returning to her own busy life. She was returning home confident and ready to take on her world by storm. After everything that she'd been through, she had nothing to fear. The future was looking great.

EPILOGUE

Lara woke up. It was the middle of the night. It had been weeks since she had returned now, but still she couldn't seem to get used to the sounds of the city. Sometimes she just lay there, thinking of the quiet of the forests of Wyoming. And then her thoughts turned to Chase.

She wanted to see him again. She needed him. But life had gotten in the way so far. They had stayed in contact, but it simply wasn't the same.

She got out of bed and walked to the window. She looked out on the city below, the city that was never at rest, not fully. She knew what she wanted to do. She stood there thinking about the forests stretching out as far as the eye could see, the mountains rising to touch the sky. And then she thought about him. Out there, trudging through the snow or hiking the foothills. Chase was there, all those long miles away from her.

And she was going to go to him.

To find out what happens to Lara and Chase next, check out Heart of Conflict – Book 2 of the Wild Hearts series!

Keep reading for a sneak peek!

HEART OF CONFLICT - DESCRIPTION

One new love. One old flame. One mistake that could change her life forever.

When Lara left Wyoming, she thought she'd found it all. Chase seemed like the man of her dreams, and for once she wasn't alone. It's a long way to Chicago, however, and sometimes not even love can bridge great distances.

Now, a year later, Lara returns to the mountains with a new love and a chance to start over. Her intensions are good, but the embers of Chase still smoulder deep in her heart. Add jealousy, chauvinism, and the clash of urban and rural life, and what's left is an explosive mix she can't hope to contain.

Can love survive the most deadly of mistakes?

Or will Lara's decision cost her everything in the end?

Heart of Conflict is a moving sweet contemporary romance that is full of love and betrayal, jealousy, and tenderness. It is perfect for reading by the beach or under your favourite tree.

This is Book 2 of the heartwarming Wild Hearts series, set in the beautiful Wyoming mountains.

SNEAK PEEK - HEART OF CONFLICT

CHAPTER 1

Lara breathed deeply as she waited. Everything over the past few weeks had been building to this moment. She knew that what happened next could have long-lasting consequences for her.

She thought back to some of the most intense times she had experienced, including those weeks when she had been out in Wyoming the first time. But then, she tried not to dwell on those days too much. For all the joy they had brought her, there was still a kind of mystical sorrow as she thought about it. About all of it. Sometimes her heart still strayed back there. On hard days, of course. On stressful days, when things seemed to pile up more and more, she would imagine herself back there, sitting on that porch in the evening just watching the sun set, or being out on a hike. Maybe on a hike with Chase.

But then, whenever a vision of him would come floating in her mind, she would feel the pain - sharp, deep within her, and had to suppress those thoughts. That was all behind her now. But she could still carry the lessons she had learned with her.

She had grown so much in that time away, learned so much about herself, became stronger than she ever thought possible.

She had returned to the city with a new vigor, a new focus and the partners at the law firm had noticed it right away. Her career had gone from strength to strength in those weeks and months that followed, and now here she was, awaiting the verdict in a case that she fought for and worked hard on.

She was proud of how she had performed in court. She felt confident. But even so, no matter how self-assured she felt, there was always going to be that moment of doubt where she wondered if she had misread things and had, in fact, gotten things wrong.

She found herself breathing deeply and then, at the last moment, holding her breath as the judge read out the verdict. She finally let her breath out in a rush as the judge announced his ruling in her favor. She slammed her hand down on the desk in front of her, and then looked to her client with a look of triumph on her face.

"We won?" he asked.

"We won," she confirmed. He stood up, smiling and shook her hand excitedly.

When she left the courthouse, she pulled her phone out of her pocket and called Mr. Peters, the partner who had assigned her the client.

It had been him who had given her the push to go to Wyoming when things had seemed as though they were about to overwhelm her. Her private life problems had seeped into her professional life to the point where she felt dangerously close to a breakdown, and she felt that his decision to reassign her was a punishment, despite his insistence that it wasn't.

But then, rather than working from home, she had gone to Wyoming. And everything had changed.

When she returned home, she was determined to ensure that the positive changes she had made would continue, that they wouldn't fade to memory. She thought it would take a conscious effort not to fall back into old habits, but in fact it had been easy. The changes had been more profound than she had realized, apparently.

But all the same, as she got back into the swing of things at the office, as she felt the pressure rise with new cases and rose to the challenges, there was a part of her that yearned to be back there - to be back in Wyoming. Back in the wild. Back with Chase.

Chase, the man who had brought something into her life that she thought she'd never have. Passion, tenderness, companionship. Someone to care for, and someone who cared for her. It had all been so magical.

But then, just as suddenly as it happened, the dream burst. What she thought was the start of something truly special and lasting had, instead, turned to ashes in her hands, leaving her reeling yet again in pain and heartache.

Now, these many months later, with a new man in her life, she still thought back to those mountain peaks so far away and her mountain man, Chase Hunter, and wondered how things had gone so wrong.

SNEAK PEEK - HEART OF CONFLICT

CHAPTER 2

When she left Wyoming, after her glorious stay, Chase had been so kind and tender.

"Let me know that you got home okay, alright?" he said to her as he closed the door to her car like a gentleman.

She smiled back at him, his kindness and thoughtfulness warming her heart, leaving her feeling like she was about to float away on a cloud. "I will, Chase, but don't worry. I'll be fine. I'm better on the road than I am on the mountain."

They both shared a laugh at this, remembering her near-disastrous mountain top fall that had brought them together.

She drove away, her eyes suddenly misting over with tears as she looked back at his smiling and waving form, disappearing like a dream around a bend on the rough gravel mountain road.

No, not like a dream, she told herself firmly. I*'m going to see him again soon, and then again after that. What we have is too special to let something as silly as distance come between us.* She told herself these words as she drove, first through the idyllic town of Sunset Ridge, and then onto the highway that carried her east, back to her life as she'd once known it. The words brought her comfort, and she savored them as the miles flew by.

As soon as she got home and walked into her downtown Chicago apartment, she felt a strange sense of familiarity tinged with something she couldn't quite identify. It was home, the chic apartment that she kept so immaculate and tastefully decorated, and yet it didn't feel like it quite fit anymore. It towered over the city below, and yet she felt strangely trapped and hemmed in. The space couldn't compare with the towering peaks, the clean air, and the absolute peace of Wyoming. She found herself missing it already, painfully. More than that, she found herself missing Chase.

She picked up the phone, as tired as she was, and called him before bed. They talked long into the night, falling asleep while on the phone, and awakening to each other. It was utterly magical.

They stayed in touch like that over the next few weeks, as best they could, calling and messaging each other when her busy schedule allowed. It was hard, however. The firm demanded her attention, and she soon found it hard to talk to Chase as much as she wanted.

Still, she enjoyed their chats, usually in the evening right before she was about to drift asleep after another long day in the courtroom. She would just lie back and listen to Chase talk about his new job – he had taken over the role of caretaker after the untimely, and terribly sad passing of the old caretaker, Clint.

There was a sense of excitement in the way Chase spoke about his work, even when he complained.

"Honestly, Lara. These city people. They really don't have a clue what they are doing," he grumbled to her. "They are just...ridiculous. There's no other word for it."

"Oh really?" Lara tried to hide the amusement in her voice. "What are they doing? Getting attacked by cougars? Almost falling off cliffs? That sort of thing?"

"No, look, that's different. That's...that's just different." His voice stuttered a bit with uncertainty, and she bit her lip to keep from laughing.

"In what way is it different? Wasn't I pretty clueless?"

She could practically hear him squirming down the phone. She quite liked doing this to him.

"I mean..." The phone went silent, Chase clearly not sure what trap she was leading him down, or what to say to extricate himself from it.

"Oh my goodness, Chase, I'm teasing you. It's fine. Calm down." She laughed out loud over the phone, enjoying that she'd gotten him going so easily.

There was a pause on the other end, and then he joined her in laughter.

"Ah! I guess you got me," he said.

She closed her eyes and she could suddenly see that smile of his, that huge smile, and she wanted it to be right there in front of her.

Suddenly, she began to feel the deep ache of loneliness and a desperate need to see him.

"Come to Chicago. Please." Her voice was almost a plea.

But she knew, that it wasn't something she could push. She knew that if it was ever going to happen, then it would have to happen in its own time, when he was ready. They were just discovering their relationship, and she knew he still suffered from the pains of his past that had driven him into the wilds in the first place.

She wasn't surprised when he said "I don't know if that's a

good idea, Lara. But someday soon, I promise". She held to that promise as she drifted off, the sound of his breathing on the other end of the line lulling her to sleep.

After that night, it didn't take long before she felt as though she had to go back, if even for a few days, and truly be with him again, without all of the miles and commitments getting between them. If he couldn't come to Chicago, then she was going to him, and that was all there was to it...

Make sure to pick up your copy of
Heart of Conflict.

Available soon on Amazon.

FREE GIFT

Want to find out what happened to Sarah, Chase's high school sweetheart?

Sign up to Kay's mailing list to receive your FREE exclusive copy of the clean and sweet romance book *Songbird,* a Sunset Ridge Novella. You'll also be notified of new releases, giveaways, contests, cover reveals and so much more.

Get your FREE copy at subscribepage.com/kaywolfebooks

A voice and guitar. A song that will open doors. A fateful night that could end it all.

With her whole life uprooted - her high school love gone, her hometown left behind - Sarah Silver decides to start over again in the big city.

Her music is what has always been there to carry her through the hard times. Now, it's caught the attention of Nashville record labels, and of a handsome mystery man who is new in town and has come to see her play.

But one mistake can ruin everything. One decision can take it all away.

Will the sweet sound of the songbird remain,
when the storm has raged and gone away?

ONE MORE THING BEFORE YOU GO...

May I ask for a small favor?

I'd love to hear what you think of this book!

Honest reviews on Amazon are incredibly helpful for other readers to decide if this is the type of book they'd enjoy, and also for authors like me to receive welcome feedback.

Your support is much appreciated!

You're the BEST!

All my love,
Kay

ABOUT THE AUTHOR

Kay Wolfe is a sweet contemporary romance and women's fiction author. Kay gives her readers strong and inspiring women who struggle through real-world challenges and in the end find love and happiness.

As a lifelong avid reader, tales of inspiring romance are Kay's passion. Nothing brings her more pleasure than living vicariously through the ebbs and flows of love, and the intricate lives of her characters. A firm believer in happy endings, she lives for the joy of seeing love prevail against seemingly impossible odds.

Drawing from her own experiences of living in small mountain towns, Kay knows the healing power of close-knit community and of nature.

Kay loves strong mochas, chocolate seashells, and lilac perfumes. She lives in a quaint little town at the foot of the Rockies, and enjoys long hikes in the mountains, picking wild berries, and curling up by the fireplace with her favorite book. She also loves to join in on occasional camping adventures with her own poet-musician husband, energetic son, and fluffy dog.

If you want to know when her next book comes out, sign up for her newsletter at subscribepage.com/kaywolfebooks.

facebook.com/kaywolfebooks
instagram.com/kaywolfebooks
twitter.com/kaywolfebooks

Manufactured by Amazon.ca
Bolton, ON

20032092R00069